# THE MAPMAKERS OF SPITALFIELDS

*Smanzuslam*
*31/10/97*

# SYED MANZURUL ISLAM

# THE MAPMAKERS OF SPITALFIELDS

PEEPAL TREE

First published in Great Britain in 1997
Peepal Tree Press Ltd
17 King's Avenue
Leeds LS6 1QS
England

ISBN 1 900715 08 2

FOR AMALIA AND TOMAL

# CONTENTS

# GOING HOME

It all began with a chance meeting at the crossroads between the Victoria and the Circle lines at King's Cross. Zamil spotted me among a cloud of jostling city-gents in grey pinstripes and brollies. Pity there are so few bowler-hats these days. They look so exotic, don't you agree? Zamil said it was easy to recognise me; my duffel coat gave me away. Both of us were a bit uneasy at meeting again. Ever since that bitter goodbye years ago, we had carefully avoided each other's shadows and haunts, used different survival-kits to get by, put on different illusions and passions and clothes, and even tried to forget the good and the bad times we had together. But how can you do that? Now we exchanged addresses eagerly, and got so carried away with gossip over who and how and what during all this time that we forgot the unpleasant circumstances that had separated us. Suddenly realising he had made himself late, Zamil had to dash off to his office in the City. Before he left he looked at me and half-whispered, as if I alone should hear his secret, *I suppose my time has come. I'm really off back home this time. You don't believe me, do you? But it's true, you know. Why don't you come to my place this Saturday, before midday – I'll tell you more.*

Despite my misgivings – and inspite of the unease that followed me through the short ride in the tube to Highgate, through the road bending northwards and lined with trees, even at the turning at the red postbox at the corner of the cul-de-sac of suburban houses with bay windows – I did go to Zamil's place that Saturday morning. It was his wife, Shapla, who opened the door.

– *Oh, it's you!* she said. She stood motionless in the frame for a few seconds, offering me that mellow icon of her face which had always reminded me of the rain-soaked tropic we called home, before turning behind a deluge of black hair. She ambled ahead of me, her plumpish figure wrapped delicately in the emerald plasticity of a silk sari, with a modesty which was as provocative as ever. A nonchalant dab of attar wafted towards me. Yes, it seemed that the mood of imminent return had added something, almost a new finesse to her step. I followed her, and on the way the familiar complaint, so ruefully drawled, yet a touch coquettish, *Have you forgotten us?* Ah the same old Shapla, who didn't seem to have changed much, but only became more the way I remembered her. My God, the children! So many of them, uproarious, sliding the banister, and cavorting in the corridor. Showing me to the lounge with a nod of her head, and biting her lips mischievously, Shapla hurried towards the kitchen. Perhaps they were half expecting me, but there they were, sitting in a semicircle in front of the fire, absorbed in the muffled buzzing of a conversation. Hearing me enter, they went quiet and turned to look at me. Under the dim, pastel-blue of the lampshade they looked as though they were just awakening from a dream. Zamil was the first to get up, then Shafique and Badal greeted me. For more than ten years they had been meeting each other, at least once a week, sometimes more often, but where had I been?

I sat next to Badal on a double settee, sinking into its soft, velvet-covered cushions. At first we looked at each other with an air of embarrassment, until, unexpectedly, Badal took me by the arm, and smiled with the relief of a man who had found something lost years ago. He asked if I remembered that day he and I shared back home – was it just before dusk or in the haze at dawn? Yes, gradually I, too, became ensnared. How could one not remember or avoid that passion for our lost place? Against our better judgements, and despite what we knew to be the reality, we plunged yet again into talking as if we had grown up in an enchanted garden. But this was not the end but the beginning of our invariable task: to recreate that fabulous home, almost element by element, paying scrupulous attention to the most minute variations, the infinite odours, and not overlooking even the most transitory of colours, the tactile surfaces of things. Zamil told me that it was simply a matter of sorting out the practicalities. You know, he said, how these things take time. But nothing would keep him here, once he had sorted them out. In the mean time, he insisted on telling me what he would do when he returned home.

Then something happened – I wasn't aware then how it came about – but I knew it was the prelude to something momentous, or that at least I was going to hear a tale in which I would find some moment of contentment. Immediately – at some invisible signal – the listeners arranged their postures as if they were preparing to give themselves completely to what was about to unfold. Shafique put a scatter cushion over the back of the settee, laid his head gently on it, closed his eyes, and began drumming his small tapering chin with his twitching fingers. Badal lurched forward, balancing his chin on the palm of his hand, which in turn rose vertically like a plinth from his right thigh. Shapla and Shafique's wife, Kalpana, came tiptoeing and stood behind their husbands, their eyes absorbed with desperate longing. Even the children seemed to have sensed the gravity of the moment and went quietly upstairs to play. Zamil had the stage to himself, and he knew it. He dragged long on his

cigarette, blew smoke through his nose with the flair of a true
virtuoso, his gaze tracing the undulating coils in the air, then
going perhaps beyond this place, beyond this time. But where?
He began by telling us that the idea had come to him as a
miraculous vision. Every detail was so clearly laid out that he
seemed to have known them all along. How there was the sweet
smell of jack-fruit, how the hum of flies had turned the key, the
jack-in-the-box of memory had jumped out and he had caught
the tune. There were lines of palm trees, surely the tall, tall tal-
palms, the nests of babuy birds hanging, as they had always
done, from their stems. There, between the flaming red of
cotton-flowers was the road he took. It had to be far from cities,
so it was far from cities. He told us how, after the rainy season,
when the rivers and fields became a vast expanse of water, one
could only reach the place by boat. At other times, trekking
through the intricate labyrinth of paddy fields would be the only
way. At first there would only be five of them, unless, of course
– he looked at me between puffs of his cigarette – I would like
to join them. My expertise would be so useful, he said. They
would buy a few plots of land, and the project would be
conceived on collective principles. Naturally, they would insist
on self-sufficiency, and everything would be like the old times
again, but only better. Wouldn't you agree, he said, looking at
me, that separation only flames a lover's heart? Ah yes, hadn't
we been nurturing our passion for our native land for years.
Moreover, with their clear vision and knowledge, how sweet
would be sweet sugar cane; the old place would pulsate with a
splendour never before seen. We would be the alchemists of the
new era, and even mud and cow-dung would glitter. But there
would have to be – the place couldn't do without it – some
special, precious spot. Yes, the place should have a circular
pond, its soft ripples festooned with the green of hyacinth. We
would cultivate tilapia, he said, the fast-breeding type – the

damn things breed even faster than our lot – crafty, yeah? If his vision was true, and he was certain it was, maybe we wouldn't need to dig a pond at all, it was probably already there, and he saw himself at dusk as the glowing disk of the sun dropped lazily, sprinkling orange on the stillness of the pool. A kingfisher, plumaged in crimson and sapphire, was waiting with infinite patience on an overhanging branch for its last meal of the day, and he too was waiting with his line flung out to count the end of another beautiful day:

*It dances today, my heart, like a peacock it dances, it dances. It sports a mosaic of passions like a peacock's tail, it soars to the sky with delight, it quests. Oh wildly it dances today, my heart, like a peacock it dances.*

Once the tale had ended, both Shapla and Kalpana, suddenly aware that their hands were resting lovingly on the shoulders of their husbands, perhaps even caressing them, withdrew them smartly. Shafique and Badal remained frozen in the same positions. It was impossible to tell whether they felt sad or quietly happy. Even Zamil, for all his lyrical exuberance, couldn't quite erase the melancholic shadows from his eyes.

Shapla and Kalpana went back to the kitchen. Lighting another cigarette, Zamil asked me what I thought of his plans. Yes, indeed, what did I think? The strange pastiche of nostalgia and the visions of alchemy made me terribly uneasy. I confess I thought that this lot were really up against it, perhaps even turning a bit potty – you know what I mean – and yet I couldn't say that I wasn't affected by it. Of course, I didn't say all that, just that cursed word which has infected me over the years – *how in-te-res-ting!*

Just past midday, Shapla called us to dinner and we soon found ourselves around the dining-table, lined with multicoloured bowls between tall glasses and smooth porcelain plates. It seemed we had stepped into a perfumed room. Ah the

obligatory hilsa fish, the real thing from the Zamuna, cooked
equally authentically, with Shapla's loving hands stirring the
paste of mustard. There were lady's fingers or okra – no, no, that
won't do, the real name is dharosh – fried lightly with garlic in
olive oil. Although nobody remarked on it, I knew that the sprats
were prepared for their uncanny resemblance to the small fishes
we could still smell on our fingers. There were other delicacies
also in deceptive simulacra. Shortly, the children came to join
us; and across the table Kalpana, between picking food from her
plate, talked to me for the first time. Badal, sensing my discom-
fort, never left my side. Perhaps being a bachelor too, he felt a
special empathy. But Shapla was always there, fussing over me
in her own enigmatic way. She looked at my plate and asked was
I too shy to help myself? So, despite my protestations, she served
me two succulent pieces of hilsa, glistening like molten silver.
We ate with passion, in silence, except for the munching
cacophony of our jaws. It was the only ritual we hadn't quite
betrayed. But we knew it wasn't quite the same, never quite the
same. Where was that humidity of the afternoon when,
despite much fanning and drinking of cool glasses of water,
we couldn't prevent the sweat from dripping endlessly from
our foreheads and dropping onto our plates. After the main
course there was only chamcham and mango to come. The
children, impatient to continue their games, hurried off with
their portions.

It was late in the afternoon. Shapla brought in a tray of home-
style aromatic tea – you know the sort – not brewed but cooked
on simmering heat and in the same pot with sugar, cardamom
and thickly-creamed milk. She went around the table serving
the tea in gilt-edged white porcelain cups – there was no need
to go through any English 'milk and sugar?' ritual. But Badal
had something else on his mind. He took a sip, put on a poker-
face and said: *Well... er... mash-potato!* That really did it.

Infectious giggles caught just about everybody, except Shapla. *You lot are really cruel*, she said. Everybody stopped for a moment, but when they looked at each other, they burst out laughing again. Shapla, still as serious as ever, said: *How can you laugh at these poor people. It isn't really their fault that they haven't learnt to eat any better, is it? Things are changing, you know. Isn't it our mission to initiate them into culinary civility? They are getting there slowly; already madrases and vindaloos have taken root. Soon other refinements will follow. You see, it's only a matter of time before we succeed in our mission, and educate their uncouth palates to become those of pukka connoisseurs. And don't forget that in the process our fellows will make a bob or two — isn't it just wonderful?*

Badal, though amused by the absurdities that Shapla was churning out of his little bit of fun, was itching to make a riposte. *Our fellows are making a few bobs, okay, okay, that's fine by me*, he said, *but all that shit these buggers are stuffing themselves with — madrases, vindaloos and what not? Would you feed that shit to your dog? Okay, okay, Shapla, whatever you say, I concede. But how about mash-potato madras or mash-potato vindaloo then?* It was Shafique who took over the cue from Badal and said: *I say, I say, old boy. A solar-hatted sahib, mad as a hatter, likes nothing better than riding on a coolie's back. But under the midday-sun he goes, riding the coolie-man on a wild boar chase with his double-barrel. He goes bang bang through the bushes, while spurring the coolie for a faster ride. Do you know what he says? God it's so funny! The hatter screams in sergeant-major-style — 'Jaldi jaldi, boy, show this damn boar, how damn well we civilised you!'* Ebbing laughter swelled again, but Shapla — who else, always so prudish and damn serious — had to be the spoilsport. *The Raj wasn't a laughing matter, you know*, she said. Zamil had a real fit at that; he was shaking precariously on the edge of his chair. Luckily, he regained his

balance just in time, and said: *Take this one, I swear it's a killer.*
*Who else but Madam Blue, the grocer's daughter, had a night-*
*mare. What did she do? Well, well, she woke up screaming. I tell*
*you something: that Madam Blue, the iron-lady, has no shame.*
*You know, she actually did it before the cameras. How obscene!*
*'Oh God!' she screamed, 'they're swamping our Shakespeare in*
*their Argy-Bargy-Paki-Woggy bog. Help! Help! Sir Francis,*
*where are you? Off with their balls, off with their balls. Nuke 'em,*
*nuke 'em.'* No doubt Zamil hadn't intended this, none of us
wanted it to end like this, but the rising hysteria of his intended
punch line knocked the laughter out of the ring. Everyone
sagged into a blank silence, except Shapla, who twitched the
corner of her lips disapprovingly.

This was how another spontaneous carnival in front of mirrors
came to an end. I knew it was better not to fall for it, but at least
the laughter, even if only momentarily, almost allowed us escape
from it all. It confirmed our lacerated alliance in this no-man's-
land. Otherwise, who knows what we would have done, perhaps
something really crazy right there and then. But soon we would
be queuing at the bus-stop, shivering in the howling sub-zero
wind. None of us would be able to avoid being squashed in the
tube between gents veiled behind their broadsheets, cultivating
aversion, and manicured ladies in sickening perfumes. Soon
night would fall and we would be hurrying to our flats with a
multitude of feet behind us, rustling with primordial terror. God,
they were everywhere, and so persistent; we weren't safe even
behind the bolted doors of our flats. They had a way of slipping
their menace into our little zones of security with the press of a
television switch or the opening of a newspaper. 'Absurd,' I hear
you say, dear brothers and sisters, 'how absurd'. Yes yes yes, I
know, how very absurd. We ought to go home, at least for our
children's sake.

We were still sitting around the table. Before us lay the

scattered skeletons of the fishes we had just consumed, devastating the order and the elegance Shapla had so zestfully arranged. We seemed not only lost for words, but also for our power of thought. Besides, the lone eye of a hilsa – whose other eye someone had sucked in along with its brain – pale and obscene in the exposed hole of its socket – had fixed an unblinking stare on me. It was only the clinking of glass bracelets, perhaps from an arm lifting a cup a bit too abruptly, that rescued me from the horror of the eye. I don't know what the connection was – it was so far back in time – but the sound was enough to summon the memories of a cool afternoon when there was nothing more than a wattle fence separating me from Shapla. She was in a white pinafore frock with pinkish flowers, sucking tamarind with chilli paste and salt, but she wouldn't give me any, only teasingly lobbing their reddish seeds over the fence. I was a bit put out, but found a way of making up for it. Through the narrow gap in the fence, I could see the seeds as they travelled to my side in gentle loops of flight. I didn't miss a single one; I caught them in the air, and ever since, almost compulsively, have been counting them. I know it's odd but each time, to my amazement, they never fail to turn up my favourite number: 9.

Despite myself, as though driven by a secret pulse of memory, I stole a sidelong glance at Shapla. How desperately I was hoping to catch a sign of something between us – nothing as vulgar as a wink of course, perhaps not even a demure flutter of eyelids, but simply a hint that for a moment would have reciprocated my old memories. But she was in no such mood, sipping away listlessly at the gilt-rimmed cup between her lips.

We went back to the lounge but the gloom still followed us from the dining room. Shapla and Kalpana went upstairs to see what the children were doing. Shafique took it upon himself to do something about the awkwardness that had silenced us. He began to lull us by recalling how one time, during the darkest night of the month, with a spear and a kerosene-lamp in his hand, he had swarmed with so many other villagers towards the swamp and its dark shallow expanses of water. For days, between heavy downpours, it had been drizzling. Everything was perfect for spear-fishing. All one needed was patience and an alert pair of eyes. It was simply a question of stooping a little, and following the patch of light cast from the hurricane-lamp, held just in front. In the pitch-black of the night, the lamps drew in fishes like swarms of insects; and they jumped in frenzy. Nothing was simpler than taking rough aim and letting go of the spear. Without fail, the spear homed in on its target, piercing a fish. On that night, among the formation of hurricane lights and the joyous exclamations of villagers passing the chillum between them, Shafique had followed the patch of light, alert even to the slightest of movements, in slow slow motion. First, he had speared a few small ones; there was laughter all around as the catch was so good that night. Then, something jumped into his patch of light, splashing water all over him. Yes, it was huge. But he was so startled he couldn't throw the spear in time, and the thing had already turned and was cruising away. He could see its fin cutting the water, but always just out of reach of his spear range. There was something strange about the thing; it seemed to have the measure of his pace even before he moved and he felt compelled to follow it, as though possessed by it. But then it had vanished the way it came. He stood up to look around. He couldn't hear a single soul in the swamp, nor see the formation of lights that had accompanied him. He had either left the others way behind or they had all gone home hours ago. Now there wasn't any doubt in his mind that the thing had led him on. He was alone in the darkness of the vast swamp, at the mercy of whatever phantoms inhabited it. Suddenly he saw a white horse leap out of the dark water and gallop towards him. Luckily he knew what to do. He held the hurricane-lamp steady and began reciting the blessed names of Allah. But he could feel the shiver as the horse kicked up a wind; it snorted violently as it ran past and disappeared into the darkness. He turned round and tried to run, but the slime of the mud-bed slowed him down. He sensed the terror of death for the first time in his life, because the phantom of the swamp had him in its power. It could take so many forms and shapes, sometimes the most enchanting, at others the most horrific. This time, a damsel, demurely dressed in white, was calling out to him. She was sweet and he almost succumbed to her charm.

While we were absorbed in Shafique's tale, he paused for a moment, spread the palms of his hands before his face and said in prayer: *Bless the holy prophet and our blessed ancestors.* Resuming the tale he told us that he knew that following the damsel in white would lead to doom. So he recited and recited the whole 99 blessed names of our omnipotent creator from the beginning to the end, and many times over. And the damsel melted into the water. He struggled on in the darkness, only protected by the blessed names, and the dim light of the hurricane lamp. The rain was coming down hard now, and something again emerged from a whirlpool of water. This time the creature had a pair of green eyes as bright as the headlights of a night-express but infinitely more ominous. It rushed towards him, grunting with a horribly shrill voice. It was so terrifying, Shafique said, that he would never forget it. But he was lucky. He ran and ran until, finally, he saw the flickering lights from the distant villages. Then he saw the bright lights of flambeaux moving through the rain and coming towards the swamp. It was the villagers looking for him. One last time the creature passed him by, then it swung around and said: 'You don't know how lucky you were today, your lamp and the names of the one I am not allowed to speak have saved you, but I warn you not to come again to the swamp when it is the darkest of nights and raining.'

Next day they found Yousef, the woodcutter, in the swamp. The poor fellow, Shafique said, unlike Shakespeare, was truly swamped – buried upside-down in the mud.

It was quite late now. The children were already sleeping upstairs. Shafique and Kalpana would stay the night. Zamil and Shapla insisted that I, too, should stay. But I accepted the offer of a lift from Badal. Shapla was sleepy, but saying goodbye at the door, she at last managed a smile for me. I was happy for that.

We drove through the cool fog of the night, down the Highgate hills, along the straight drive through Archway, and turning left, towards Finsbury Park. On the way, Badal told me that the tale of the creature of the swamp was Shafique's speciality. Apparently, he had first told the same tale more than ten years ago, when he joined the group. Ever since he had been repeating it, many times, but always a shade different. For instance, Badal told me, the month before, it wasn't a horse at all but a tiger that leapt out of the water, and further back, the night was moonlit rather than the darkest and so on. But, you know, Badal continued, despite hearing it so many times, it was strange how he never get tired of Shafique's tale. And despite knowing the plot so well, and anticipating its changes, he still allowed himself the suspense of terror, as though he were hearing it for the first time. But there was more to it than that, and perhaps it was this other reason that kept him tied to the tale's monotonous repetition. Each time, he said, he was touched by something he couldn't quite explain, yet the force of that touch was real enough; and it kept him going for all those years. *I know things were never like this*, he said, *and perhaps I'm a bit deluded, but every time I hear Shafique's tale, I can't help myself but give in to the notion that it captures the essence of our lost memories, say, of the pattering of drizzle and of the pitch-blackness of nights.*

*How else but by tracing their oblique lines,* he said, *can I walk once more the muddy road in the pitch-black nights, hurricane-lamp in one hand and an umbrella in the other. In those monsoon nights, do you remember, I used to visit your house at the other end of the village. It is so good to see you again,* he continued, *I hope one day I can take the same road again to see you at the other end of the village.* When we arrived at my flat in Finsbury Park, Badal reminded me that the next week's gathering would be at Shafique's. *You haven't really got to know Kalpana yet. She is the most passionate among us about going home.*

That night I slipped into bed, propped against the pillow and set myself, as I habitually do, the task of reading a book and falling asleep. I opened the page by pulling the marker; it was 249. K.R, the immaculate logician, had remorselessly pieced together the jigsaw. Now he knows the next move the artful fiend is about to make, and sets his stratagem with the same customary inevitability. In two more pages a face and a name will be revealed, perhaps a bullet through his temple and blood splattered on a marble floor. Or perhaps, finally, it would be K.R. himself, caught up as he was in the smouldering passion of his own logic, who would be entangled in the linear thread, between the black and white coolness of rhombic tiles. Did it really happen like this? Who knows, because I can't remember the rest, perhaps I had already fallen asleep.

London is our city, so let us take the city. Four of us, our lapels turned up in our matching macintoshes, are out on an evening saunter. We are having a good time, a happy-go-lucky, enjoy-ing-our-mates-time, our faces camouflaged in a thickening mist-time. *Who's there,* we say to ourselves in whispers, at a bend between tall buildings. We hear a group of our American cousins savouring a good tourist time. No, they are not coming this way, oh yes, they are coming this way. Sensing our presence,

one of the guys says: *Gee! we kinda love your fog, pal*. What can
we do but stay quiet, pulling our trilbies down a bit. The
American comes in for a closer look, almost breathing into our
faces. What does he see? Surely not the brothers of Sherlock
Holmes, as he expects. He sees only brown fellows turning away
their faces in the mist. Finally it dawns on the guy that he is
seeing the wrong sort of cousins and pals. He breaks into a run
and we hear him saying – *Holy shit! Gee! Gee!* – as he disappears
into the mist. We are not ruffled by the incident. We know the
streets, so we cut corners, side-walks, into alleyways, enjoying
our misty anonymity again. We light fags in automatic syn-
chrony and whistle the same tune. It's time to look for a tea-stall
for a hot cuppa, snacks of samosas, and perhaps some chit-
chats. But there is a blind spot, an open manhole, and we slip
through, falling into the maze of sewers, into the belly of London.
We don't fall like Alice, because migrants like us don't fall like
Alice. But we have fallen into a subterranean darkness, where
tunnels forms labyrinths from which one can't escape by simply
opening one's eyes and waking up. But we don't panic. Because
London is our city, and we know the city. We lock our arms
together and we grope along, almost inch by inch, through the
tunnels. The rats, so many and so huge, scuttle about, disturbed
by the splashing of our weary feet. Then we hear the murmur of
liquid shit, running through a tunnel near by. My God, the smell!
So many gaping mouths! There is a tunnel full of shit gushing
towards us. Which one? Which one? To our relief, suddenly,
there is the simplicity of a single tunnel, clearly marked: Way
Out. More confident, we stride along, our arms locked, Zamil
leading the way. Then we hear the monotonous tones of a tour-
commentator speaking through a loudspeaker. Sensing our
presence, he changes his tune. Most amicably he says, *Welcome,
gentlemen*. We feel pleased. Then, without changing his amica-
ble tone, he says: *So few are as lucky as you, gentlemen; you've*

*hit upon the ancient one-way street, leading to our magnificent heritage, the famous/infamous towers of the black ravens. You see, long before your time, only our treacherous nobles came this way. Now you, intrepid travellers, or shall I say archaeologists – but let me be the first to congratulate you, gentlemen. Have a jolly good time*, he says, laughing like the black ravens in the towers. Before we get our bearings back and lock our arms again, a wind has blown up. Zamil tries to light a match but its flicker is blown out each time. We see that the liquid shit is swelling like waves and gushing towards us along the tunnel. In the panic of the moment, we forget that it is our city. We get scattered and break into a run in the dark. But waves of shit rush in faster than we can run. God! What a smelly way to go!

Then I heard the telephone ring. It was early morning, the time when during weekdays the morning rush hour would already have begun. That day it was so quiet.

It was Badal; he was trembling as he spoke. He told me that Zamil had suffered a severe heart attack that morning; he had been taken to an intensive care unit. I reached the hospital at about 8 o'clock; the others were already there. Badal, Shafique, and I sat together in the waiting room. Kalpana was standing, propped against the windowsill, thin and diminutive, her head slightly tilted to the left, the curls of her hair falling over her breast and only partially covering her right cheek. If her right index finger hadn't been looping her hair she would have cut an elegant statuette in mournful relief. Of course, they allowed Shapla to go with Zamil. Badal passed me a cigarette; Shafique broke the silence. You know, he said, I had a dream last night, in which we slipped through a manhole. Badal looked at Shafique and nodded as if he too had the same dream. I thought that if Shapla knew about our mysterious empathy, this singular and unison dream, she would have been so annoyed. Hours passed by sitting, smoking cigarettes, drinking tea, and occasionally walking up to the reception and politely inquiring for news. But as yet there was no news. Suddenly, Shafique had had enough of this; he insisted on seeing the doctor. The way Shafique took charge left me in no doubt that, in Zamil's absence, he would be the natural leader. A nurse who had just come to the reception led Shafique down the corridor. Within a few minutes he was back. From his face we could tell that the news was very bad indeed. Doctors were trying their best, Shafique told us, but they wouldn't give any guarantees. Kalpana moved from the window and sat next to me, her long fingers drumming the edge of the yellow plastic bench on which we sat. She hadn't put on any attar. Then she stopped her drumming and without looking at me said, *You came just in the nick of time to take Zamil's place. We mustn't stop here, there's so much to remember and so much to plan, isn't there? You know the place Zamil told us about last night, he is surely about to return there now, I can feel it in my bones. One day we all must return there, we can't leave Zamil all alone, can we?* Badal offered me another cigarette. Shafique moved to stand behind Kalpana and placed his hands over her shoulders. She, in turn, moved her right hand diagonally across her chest to touch his fingers. He gently squeezed them, and then almost absent-mindedly, he began to stroke her hair. He stopped abruptly, and those of us who were seated stood up to receive Shapla. Strangely, despite the sadness of the moment and the dignity with which she conducted herself, her lips still had a twist which was deeply sensual.

Seeing us all, Shapla smiled delicately, shedding the burden of memories and dreams. She looked so relieved, almost happy in a way I couldn't explain. I knew that Shapla was going home.

We applied ourselves strenuously; and within days the coffin, the special arrangements with the airline which was to carry the dead body and other formalities were done. On the day,

we arrived at the airport hours before the flight, and some of their
other friends, whom we didn't know, were also there to see off
Zamil and Shapla and their three children. Seeing Shapla all
alone, and gripped by the memories of old times, I almost said
something foolish and sentimental to her. But seeing her so aloof
I knew it was neither the place nor the time for that. So I didn't
say anything to her. No special goodbyes, no tears. Shapla
simply said: *See you soon* – and disappeared behind the barrier,
out of our lives and out of this ghost dance. Yes Shapla, *See you
soon*, I said.

Before leaving the airport we had tea together. Each of us
were drowned in our separate thoughts, until Shafique, consci-
entious as ever, broke the ice. He said that minutes before it was
all over, Zamil told Shapla the name of the place where he would
like to rest. Yes, it was far away from cities, and after the rainy
season, when rivers and fields become one vast expanse of
water, you could only reach it by boat; at other times, trekking
through the intricate labyrinth of paddy fields would be the only
way. You know, Shafique said, if there was one thing Zamil
couldn't stand, it was the idea of solitude. Naturally, he wanted
to have his own father and mother, grandfather and grandmother, and in turn, their fathers and mothers and so on, beside
him. And together, they would be expecting flakes of cotton,
dead petals and leaves strewing their way, season after season
to eternity, sons and daughters, and their grandchildren too.
Kalpana puckered her lips and, curling her hair with her right
index finger, she said with a hint of bitterness, *I thought the plan
included us, all of us, in the same place*. Badal said that in a way
Zamil had included all of us, because he knew that when we
spoke of our collective plans, each of us was redrawing a
palimpsest of our own memories. *It is always like that, Kalpana*,
he said, *always beside our fathers and mothers. You see, we have
no other elements to dream with, have we?* We finished our tea

and made ourselves ready for the same old routine again —
clock-time, black-time, brown-time — licking a living from this
shit-hole and, dare I say, loving it, dear brothers and sisters. I
hear you say: *Damn fool, you never learn, do you?* Before we left
the airport, Kalpana smiled sweetly and reminded me that the
next gathering would be at her place. She said she would cook
catfish specially for me. Yes, I said, I would be there. You see,
it's the only way we can avoid being swamped on the margins.
If you think it's a pathetic delusion, you would be right, but what
else can we do?

   Since I had been taking the same route for years, I could
easily have changed lines at King's Cross with my eyes closed
then, swept along by the rushing crowd, could have crossed the
Piccadilly line platform and still could have arrived on time to
take the Metropolitan line. But on that day something unex-
pected came over me, and instead of going to work, I decided to
walk back to my flat in Finsbury Park. I took the Caledonian
Road in the rain. On the way I thought of the years I had spent
meeting Badal, Shafique and Kalpana, and dreaming of that
elusive moment of going home. Perhaps that moment wasn't far
away when I would really do it. Of course, Badal, Shafique, and
Kalpana would come to see me off at the airport. At the other end,
Zamil, my good friend Zamil, still bound by the complicity of
that fateful night, would come to receive me. I bet he would
whisper in my ear: *My dear fellow, it was damn easy; your
ridiculous winding sheet gave you away. Funny, of all people it
had to be you to follow my footsteps*, and add rather mischievously, *After all those years in England I was almost expecting
you in a bowler-hat.*

# THE ULTIMATE RIDE IN A PALANQUIN

When the messenger from the country knocked on the door with a slight tap of his knuckles, everyone except Tuku was huddled under their embroidered quilts, thinking it must be the tinkle of an elephant's bell in their flights of dreams. Tuku was wide awake in his dark bedroom, on a net-curtained bed, blowing imaginary bubbles with hazy rainbows in them. He dived, leapt and danced to catch them melting on his palms. Yet the caress of sleep would not touch his eyelids. Restless, he began another game: unravelling the cord on a top with a jerk, scooping it onto his palm and letting it spin until it swayed from side to side like a hypnotist's dangling clock. When he heard the knock, he took his eye off the top's mesmeric whir and drew his head inside the quilt, feigning deep sleep.

The messenger knocked harder. Cousin Arifa, the night owl of the house, with ever so sensitive eardrums, got up to switch on the light. She walked unhurriedly to the front door and demanded to know who it was before she opened up. Surat Ali came in, almost whispering, apologetic for his intrusion at this late hour, but his message was urgent. Tuku pricked up his ears to get wind of the message but neither Surat Ali nor Cousin Arifa spoke further.

Mother was now up and rushing towards the front door, yelling; Father, though, dazed at being woken up so suddenly, was still groping for his spectacles lost somewhere in the white linen of his bed.

Surat Ali remained respectfully silent as cousin Arifa relayed the message. Mother burst into wailing and Tuku's baby sister Sulekha, poor Sulekha, responding to Mother's distress, screamed piercingly. But suddenly there was silence, perhaps because Father had at last found his spectacles and his bearings and was telling Mother: *A coma isn't the end, believe you me. Many have returned from there and lived long lives*. Mother would have had looked at Father with a peculiar kind of credulity, holding Sulekha tightly against her breast as if in relief that the danger had passed. She knew, though, that at grandmother's age to return from a coma would be a miracle.

Feeling a sudden chill, Tuku curled himself up, but he could do nothing to prevent the frostiness of the night from creeping in through the quilt. He thought of his grandmother, of her pleated face, her toothless smile, her nimble but stooping movements supported by her short, twisted, snake-like stick, of how she laid out jars of pickles in the sun, and scooped treacle from an ochre urn onto his plate and let him suck her sugary fingers, and of her saying lovingly, *You're as greedy as your mother when she was a child*.

At least an hour must have passed before cousin Arifa came to his room, gently caressing his face with her soft hand, saying in a muffled voice, *Get up. You're to go to the village with Aunty*. Pretending to have woken from deep sleep, Tuku squirmed, moving from side to side, rubbing his eyelids. Already, long before cousin Arifa had come to him, he had got the whiff of the country – the sweet decaying smell of jute stalks rotting in the swamps, the fumes from the disks of dried dung burning in the thatched huts, and the scents of peepal, banyan, cotton, krisnachura, palms, and of the pale purple flowers swaying above the floating clumps of hyacinth. As always he would be there in the late afternoon, slingshot in hand, hunting birds with Modu, Bulu and Afzal. They would begin by tracking across the paddy fields and the swamp, but soon they would find themselves in the forest; and he would be scared of getting lost in its humid darkness as the hissing of snakes and the howls of jackals jarred its lethargic hum.

Mother interspersed packing with fits of sobbing, as if the spell of Father's assurance had worn off. He remained seated, pensive, on the edge of the bed as if at a loss as to what to do. Sulekha couldn't be persuaded to sleep again; she was crawling all over the room. When mother saw Tuku standing in the doorway, all short pants, skinny legs and chattering teeth, she hugged him and wailed. Father brushed off the still burning ash that dropped from his pipe onto his lap and said that he wasn't able to go because it would be impossible to get leave at such short notice. Mother would go with Tuku and Sulekha; Surat Ali, of course, would be the guide. As there was no time to lose, they decided to take the next train to Soranpur. Hours before the train was due, two rickshaws were called. Still sobbing, Mother climbed into one of them with Sulekha and Tuku; Surat Ali and the luggage went in the other. Father came down from the veranda to say goodbye. He dipped under the bonnet of the rickshaw to cuddle Sulekha; he tapped Tuku on the shoulder. He looked at Mother and said, *I bet when you reach the village you'll see your mother up and about, making palm bread and slaughtering swans. She's a tough nut, your mother.* The rickshaws pulled away and soon they were scuttling through the empty streets. The wind lapped against their faces and despite being huddled against Mother, Tuku felt cold; his teeth chattered again.

When they reached Mymensingh Junction, Tuku stopped feeling cold. Despite the late hour, the station was brightly lit and buzzing with people. Mother went to the waiting room with

Sulekha; Tuku walked around the station with Surat Ali. He saw magazine shops displaying colourful covers under gas lights, families cooking on open fires, coolies buried under their loads, and rows and rows of people sleeping on the platform. He followed the railway track with his eyes and saw it disappear into the darkness. He was gripped by panic. He remembered the horrible, bottomless toilets on trains and the view they gave of the dizzying blur of sleepers running on the endless tracks below. What was worse, today he had to travel with Mother in a ladies' compartment. Suddenly he rushed to the toilet at the far end of the platform. He stood there for a long time in the acrid smell of urine, but nothing happened – not even a tiny drop. Surat Ali kept asking him if anything was wrong. Tuku assured him that he just wanted to get on the train well prepared. Seeing the time on the big platform clock, they hurried back from the toilet, but the train was late as usual. Passing the station guard, Surat Ali paused to offer him a bidi and asked him what time the four-thirty was due. The station guard looked annoyed, perhaps expecting a foreign cigarette, but he took the bidi and said, *What kind of question is that, you bumpkins? Of course, the four-thirty is due at four-thirty give or take an hour. Or may be only half an hour if you're lucky*. Surat Ali was angry. He said that the guard would lick a paisa even from a pile of shit. But they were lucky; the train arrived at five o'clock. Mother, with Sulekha in her arms, and Tuku following behind, jostled into a female compart-ment with grilled windows. There were some vacant spaces on a long bench in the middle of the compartment and they sat there squashed among women with babies sprawled on their laps. Although he didn't show it, Tuku felt disappointed about not being able to sit by the window: he would miss the view of the train bending its caterpillar body, the plumes of vapour trailing from the engine, and the splinters of charcoal getting in his eyes. But he remembered his grandmother and slumped back into his seat from where he could only gaze at the pallid yellow of the cabin or the black-veiled women pressing their faces against the grills on the windows. Surat Ali waved from the platform and shouted that he was taking a seat three wagons away.

When the station bell rang and the guard waved his flag, the train whistled, pulled its giant pistons and hissed out a dense cloud of steam. At first it moved slowly, but soon gathered pace as it left the confines of the town and emerged into open country. Although there aren't more than twelve stations between Mymensing and Soranpur, the journey is a long one – it takes the whole day. Sulekha lay asleep. Mother prayed and sobbed endlessly, rocking her head to the lateral jerks of the train. Finding nothing to occupy his mind, Tuku closed his eyes, listening the train's rhythmic sound...

*It was after the midday meal; Tuku had laid his mat under the bakul tree. He was falling asleep in the slight breeze that rustled the leaves. But out of the corner of his eye he saw the sly old angel of death stealthily climbing the fig tree on the other side of the pond. How could he miss that old rascal whose reflection was rippling in the pond for all to see as he hauled himself up from a lower branch to hide in a leafy canopy? Tuku got up, crawled stealthily through the tall grasses, and rolled into the pond. Then he dived under the water to reach the other bank, and lying low among the reeds, he slipped into the undergrowth. Cocky as ever with his bagful of cunning plans, the angel was resting, his legs dangling from a branch. Still keeping silent, Tuku nimbly climbed the fig tree. Once among the branches he suddenly broke their leafy shields to surprise the angel. In his arrogance, the angel wasn't expecting anything of the sort. He was so startled when he saw Tuku that he nearly fell out of the tree. Tuku laughed and asked him, 'Why all this snooping around?' By now the angel had somewhat regained his composure and said in his usual cocky tone, 'Look, mate, I've nothing against you people*

*personally, but your grandmother's time is up, I had to come for
her.' He was still feeling a bit embarrassed about being caught
off guard by a mere child, so he made a quick exit. No sooner had
the angel left than Tuku scampered down the fig tree and ran to
the inner courtyard where Grandmother was peeling a pineapple
on the veranda. He said, breathless and stammering, 'I saw the
angel of death in the fig tree; he has come for you.' 'Let the old
fool come! Did he tell you about his cunning plan?' said
Grandmother, laughing mischievously. 'No,' said Tuku. 'His
cunning plan, my foot; it took me less than the time to spit to work
it out,' she said, now chopping the peeled pineapple into small
cubes. 'Perhaps you've guessed we'll be eating chicken curry with
pineapple tonight, but you see no chicken. Why is that so?' 'I
don't know, Grandmother,' answered Tuku. 'Because the old fool
will be coming in the guise of a black hen to gain entry into my
house. But look at the trap I've set at the door, so we'll have our
chicken for the curry,' said Grandmother, bursting into cackling
laughter.*

A sudden commotion, the whistle of the engine, and the rush
of the passengers rustling their holdalls awoke Tuku. He knew
that the train was approaching a station. When he opened his
eyes, he saw soft shafts of morning light falling within the
compartment through the chinks between the veiled women and
the window grills. Gradually the train slowed and crawled to a
halt at the platform. As he expected, it was Goripur Junction,
where the engine would leave the wagons to fill its belly with
water, before reconnecting again. He knew that the next stage of
the journey involved a long haul up. Already Tuku could hear
the hawkers frantically jingling their wares from window to
window, promising the delights of the winter. Many of the rice
bread and boiled eggs sellers climbed into the compartments to
force themselves on the passengers. But the palm juice sellers,
perhaps being novices at the art of selling, stayed outside; they

ran beside the windows with round pitchers on their heads. Knowing that he wouldn't be able to buy anything today, Tuku felt a bitter disappointment that turned into a fuming anger. He sat glum-faced, biting his nails in silence. All around him, the women in the compartment were cracking boiled eggs against the wooden seats and window frames. Despite his determination to ignore them, he couldn't prevent his nose from flaring up at the smell of the egg yolks tanged with salt and the steam of cracked rice breads. If things had been different, Tuku would have happily become a damn nuisance, pestering Mother until she gave in. But how could he ask for anything now without appearing downright greedy, a shameless child. He was so desperate that he almost told Mother that he knew all about it, that there was no need to worry about Grandmother, that she had enough wit about her to take care of the angel of death. But seeing Mother clasping Sulekha tightly to her bosom, her eyes red with dried-up tears, he kept quiet and once more stared aimlessly at the floor. He felt so bored that he pretended to doze off again. Now, there were even some vacant places by the window, but he couldn't bring himself to propose a move, so they remained seated in the middle of the carriage. By now Tuku was beginning to feel angry with Grandmother; how could she spoil the pleasure of his trip by playing this no good game with the angel of death?

Sulekha woke up and Mother gave her a bottle. She gave Tuku some rice cereal which he lazily chewed with nibbles of the date-palm gur. After drinking her bottle, Sulekha struggled to get down and crawl, but Mother desperately held on to her. Perhaps sensing the tragedy behind Mother's watery eyes, a young woman offered to carry Sulekha. She walked her up and down the aisle humming a lullaby.

Sitting next to Mother was a fat lady, all fancily dressed up and weighed down in gold and silver. She was deftly opening a

multilayered tiffin carrier, crammed with parathas and auber-
gine bhaji. Oblivious to everybody around her, and between
noisy burps and endless squelching of her tongue, she began
stuffing herself shamelessly. Perhaps it was the buzzing of a fly
or simply the smell of death that made her look at the mournful
figure of Mother beside her. Suddenly her mood changed, as if
she had become aware of the watery gaze and the bad luck it
might bring on her. She began to mumble, her mouth stuffed with
food, which spluttered all over Tuku. Mother got the message
and sobbed with gratitude but shook her head again and again.
As if almost on the verge of a panic attack, the woman pushed
the open container towards Tuku, pleading with him to dip his
hand into it. *Eat eat eat, my good boy, eat plenty, until your
stomach is exceedingly full*, she said. He looked away from her
but he couldn't help thinking how mouth-watering the food
looked – puris fried in pure butter and succulent aubergines
done to a perfect gold. He didn't need to look up to feel that all
the eyes in the compartment were turned on him as if to witness
a soon-to-be committed sin. Besides, in her rasping voice he
could hear a dim echo of the angel of death. He decided that he
wasn't going to fall for it even though his taste buds were
insisting that he should.

Suddenly there was a jolt; the engine had reconnected and
was ready to set off again. It reminded Tuku of his father, of their
previous journeys together. How father used to wait until the last
moment, until the train had already begun moving, and only
then jump on, hanging loosely by the handle bar. Father's antics
used to scare Mother no end, but Tuku always found them
amusing, because they signalled the thrills of adventure and the
promises of the country. Not forgetting, of course, those S-
shaped cookies Father always brought in his pocket from the
stalls. Soon the train gathered speed, but Tuku had to contend
with the same monotonous lack of view. Just as before, only the

metallic rotations of the wheels against the rail kept him company, bringing back to him again that afternoon of hunting with Modu, Bulu and Afzal.

*Finally, after hours of tracking, his sling shot hit the target, a forbidden bird, black with red fringes; it dropped dead underneath a jackfruit tree. He dangled the bird by its legs, ran through the rattan bush, and entered the inner courtyard where Grandmother was pounding betel nuts in a mortar – oh she hasn't enough good teeth, that's for sure. Knowing full well Grandmother's crafty ways, Tuku cautioned her from a distance: 'I swear it's forbidden, absolutely haram, even the mullah told me so.' Grandmother smiled mischievously, dipped her finger into the tamarind jar, enticing him near. She said, 'Haram, halal, forbidden/unforbidden, what kind of nonsense you talk, boy. Them silly things don't apply to me. Did I tell you of the magic words that I treasure in my skull? When I need them I just munch them and spit. All forbiddenwallas run for their lives. Are you turning into a serious type like your mother or what?'*

It was around three o'clock in the afternoon when the train arrived at the sleepy, red-bricked station of Soranpur. As soon as the train came to a halt, they had to rush to get off, because trains stop here for no more than a minute or so. Without paying any attention to anything around her, Mother headed towards the exit. Tuku, though, paused at the whistle as the train set off, throwing vapour trails behind it. Surat Ali came running to tell Mother that the palanquin would be waiting outside, under the shade of a nim tree.

Sure enough, six lean and tall men with luxurious moustaches sat under the nim tree, puffing their bidis. With their pensive faces and transparently pale brown eyes it was as if, somehow, they weren't there, but in another land. Tuku hadn't seen them before. He wondered from where on earth these men might have come to bear the palanquin. Mother hardly noticed them but Surat Ali felt that he had to explain to her that the old palanquin bearers had left the country and the new ones came from a strange land.

— *I admit they look a bit peculiar,* he said, *but nothing to worry, your respectful bibi. These fellows are good, very good. In fact, nothing less than super class at their task. I believe even the rickshaws can't keep up with them, your respectful bibi.*

Mother wasn't listening to Surat Ali; she just plodded her way towards the nim tree with Sulekha in her arms. Between the men and their two equally strange-looking lean and tall dogs stood the familiar palanquin with its painted hennaed palms of would-be brides in crimson, scattered among crescents and stars and arabesque patterns.

Mother opened the sliding door in the middle of the palanquin and urged Tuku to go in first. Then she crouched a little and entered the palanquin herself. She sat at its head with her legs spread out diagonally across the carpeted floor, leaning against a round pillow. Tuku sat at the rear with his knees folded, facing the small rectangular window with circular holes. Suddenly the dogs began to whine and bark and the men, with a jerk and a swing, snatched the palanquin up into the air. Forming straight lines, three men at the front and three at the back, they began to move without a word between them as if everything were prearranged, drilled to the minutest precision. Excited, the dogs raced ahead, came back in a loop but raced off again. Surat Ali and a porter with the luggage were walking behind. From the station compound the palanquin veered right, went down the slope and zipped through the market. As the palanquin passed, the vendors and their customers looked up with suddenly sad faces, the noisy tall-tale gossipers lounging by the tea-stall paused in silence, and even the doped-up fakirs under the banyan woke from their meditation to exhale a mournful air. From the market, the palanquin turned left and climbed the rail track that ran straight until it met the blue sky in the distance. Because it meant that no time would be wasted on the ferryboat, they were going to cross the river by the railway bridge. Sensing a change of direction, the dogs began barking again and continued to bark until the palanquin settled on the narrow single-track pathway along the rail line. Already there were many people on the pathway, but those who found themselves in front either climbed onto the rail track or down the slope to make room for the palanquin to pass. From inside, Tuku followed the humming of the fishermen as they approached, perfectly balancing themselves on a single rail, then disappeared in the distance with huge wicker baskets on their heads. When the time came to cross the bridge Tuku held his breath, closed his eyes, remembering the chasms between the sleepers. He moved close to Mother who held him like a little baby and began to pray loudly. Sulekha was asleep on the floor wrapped in a quilt. The palanquin bearers still didn't say a word between them but the dogs whined and barked as they leapt from sleeper to sleeper across the bridge.

On the other side of the bridge they came down the slope to the right again. It was late in the afternoon and the air was mellow under the soft winter sun. The mud road they took was nearly empty except for an odd bullock cart or a lonely traveller making unhurried progress. Now the palanquin was set in a rhythm, moving slightly faster than before, and the bearers, as if prompted by the loneliness of the sky, suddenly joined in a synchronised murmur. From inside, bending forward, Tuku angled his head to look out. He looked through the circular holes in the window and saw the bearers moving; their heels sprinkling clouds of dust into the air. They looked as pensive as ever with their pale brown eyes; and the dogs were still running ahead and looping back again. Surat Ali and the porter couldn't be seen anywhere – evidently they couldn't keep up with the pace and had fallen behind. Finally Tuku asked Mother what he had been meaning to ask for quite some time.

— *Where on earth are the palanquin bearers from, Mother? What do you call these people?*

Mother shook her head, looking slightly worried.

— *I don't know. Perhaps from a far far land.*

Mother looked at Tuku and began to sob again, biting the border of her sari. Now Sulekha got up screaming. Mother, between sobs, began humming a lullaby. She thought that Sulekha was hungry and made a bottle of milk, using the water from the flask. But Sulekha couldn't be consoled; she screamed and screamed. Tuku felt the anxiety he always felt when Sulekha screamed. Mother tapped on the door; the palanquin came to a halt and descended to the ground. Mother arranged her veil and came out of the palanquin. She was pacing about trying to console Sulekha. Tuku walked behind, following her every step, biting his nails. Oblivious to Sulekha's screaming, the palanquin bearers squatted huddled together by a wild creeper bush, smoking their bidis. Suddenly, after a moment's hesitation, and fretfully looking around, they closed themselves into a tightly-knit circle. After that they bent their heads, and one of them produced, as if plucking from thin air, some dough-like food and placed it on a rag of muslin. No sooner had he done this than they began to eat that food with pieces of raw onion. But they kept the secret of their tongues to themselves, only their jaws pouncing on the onions betrayed their presence. Seeing them eat, the dogs looked hungry and began to bark. One of the men turned around from the circle and threw some of the dough-like food for the dogs. Vying with each other, the dogs scampered away; they licked the food with pleasure and wagged their tails. From behind a banana grove a woman suddenly appeared with a jug full of water. Mother washed Sulekha's face and the woman cooed, making silly faces. Soon Sulekha was calm again and they got back into the palanquin. As before, and still without a word between them, the men hauled the palanquin up with a snatch.

It didn't take long for the men to regain their rhythm as they crooned in unison, and soon the palanquin was gently undulating and cutting through the air like autumnal leaves. Tuku resumed his seat by the rectangular window and looked out. As the palanquin moved, his eyes lingered on the soft light of the late afternoon playing on the fields of mustard. He wished that this flow of endless yellow would never end. Sulekha looked happy; she was making baby noises and crawling on the floor. Mother was also looking out at the sea of yellow. Despite her blank eyes she looked calm. Tuku looked into the distance, across the fields of mustard, and saw children flying kites that buzzed like planes. When they saw the palanquin they came running in a frantic relay, but stopped some distance away from it. Looking at each other they stood in silence, and then ran back the way they had come. Why? Perhaps they had sensed the gloom inside the palanquin, or perhaps they were scared off by the sight of the strange palanquin-bearers from an unknown land. Seeing them panic, the dogs barked and gave chase, but they came back as soon as one of the bearers gave a soft whistle. Although he tried to put it out of his mind, the frightened eyes of the children unsettled Tuku. For a moment he had a strange vision of himself as a captive led to slaughter in a cage. But the mesmeric murmurs of the men, the pendulous dance of the palanquin and the ceaseless yellow of the mustard returned him to ease. He leant on the round pillow against the back plank of the palanquin with his eyelids closing on him. *No, not the bloody angel again.* He heard him whispering through the planks of the palanquin. As if sensing his victory, and cocky as ever, the angel was repeating the same malicious name of death. *Bloody hell*, thought Tuku, *what a devious, no good type this angel is. He doesn't give up, does he?*

Without warning, a cold wind rattled the loose shutter of the window; it let a chill dampness into the palanquin. Gooseflesh rose on Tuku's bare legs and he woke up in an icy shiver. Sulekha was sleeping on the floor wrapped in a quilt. Mother looked the same mournful figure in the evening's approaching darkness. Outside, the purple of the haze was blurring the endless yellow of the mustard. Far in the distance, across the fields, the contours of the tall lines of trees seemed to sway their black matted locks as if in a dance of demons. But the palanquin accelerated as if winging its way through thin air. Now almost at one with the palanquin, the smooth, silky murmurs of the men were getting fainter and fainter. Everything was colluding with the silence of the evening so that the subtle music of the bearers' footsteps delicately touching the ground could now be heard. Even the dogs seemed to have caught the mood: no longer barking but only whining gently at a rhythm that kept a perfect harmony with the even pace of their paws.

When Mother saw Tuku shivering in the cold, she put a jumper on him, covered him with a quilt and arranged his tousled hair with her cold fingers. Suddenly remembering that he had hardly eaten anything the whole day, she insisted that he should have some rice cereal. But he said he wasn't hungry any more. Perhaps sensing some danger in the darkness of the night, Mother leant forwards to close the windows. Tuku pleaded with her to keep them open and she went along with him. Head turned slightly to the left, Tuku kept his eyes fixed on the lights fluttering from distant villages. Without moving, let alone looking at Mother, he asked, *Is grandmother dead?* Mother was taken aback by the suddenness of his question. She remained quiet for a while but soon she embraced him and wailed.

– *No, no she can't die without seeing you. She'll wait for us, Tuku, she will.*

Instead of being reassured, he became more anxious, and began to bite his nails. Almost stammering, he said:

– *If grandmother dies, I suppose, we won't be riding on a palanquin any more. Is it the last time we'll be coming to the country, Mother?*

Mother didn't wait to hear what Tuku was saying; she had already begun to bang her head against the side planking and broke into wailing again. Tuku touched her hand and she became quiet.

Abruptly, not far from a ruined brick-build palace that lay inside an ashen mango grove, the meandering mud road came to an end. Turning left, and down the slope, the men took a long thin ridge between the fields of paddy. Sensing that something was wrong and breathing heavily as though on the verge of panic, Mother sat up straight and opened her side of the window. She screwed her eyes as if to see the dim landscape through of the fast approaching darkness.

– *Oh Allah, did you see that, Tuku? Bearers have taken the wrong turn. Near the ruined palace, they should've turned right. Allah, why would they do a thing like that? Who are they, anyway? What do they want?*

Despite himself, Tuku couldn't help Mother's panic from leaking into him. But it passed as soon as she had stopped talking, because the bearers had already cast their magic spell on him.

– *Mother, you always worry about nothing,* he said calmly. *Perhaps they're just taking a short cut.*

Mother went quiet and both of them looked out at the misty night devouring the remains of the day. Now nothing could be seen except a few lonely flickers. But the men didn't stop to light their flambeaux as palanquin bearers usually do at night. It seemed that somehow they knew the lay of the land so well that they could trot with the same unfaltering rhythm as before, even though the darkness was total now and the path was no more than the narrow ridges between the paddies. Mother closed her side of the window.

— *I know by heart every bend of this land*, she said. *So many times, yes, so many times, I've travelled this way on a palanquin. I know it can't be a short cut, Tuku. These creatures are taking us somewhere else.*

Tuku swung like a pendulum between Mother's sense of doom and the onwards movement of the palanquin. If for a moment a menacing shiver ran through his veins, it was soon dispelled by the palanquin's spell. But he continued to look at the dancing flickers moving through the darkness. He thought he saw among them the dim, swaying lanterns of night travellers. Who were they? Who it was had told him he couldn't recall, but he remembered that country-people went to operas and the meetings of duelling poets on winter nights. Perhaps the lanterns belonged to them.

— *Nothing to worry, Mother*, he said. *I know they'll take us to Grandmother's home. They know how to get there; they do it all the time. Don't they?*

Mother didn't listen to his reassuring words. She began to knock on the door. Immediately the dogs started to bark threateningly, and the palanquin abruptly came to a halt, but remained suspended in the air. A guttural voice came to the door and muttered something in a strange language and went back to his position. Silent again, they moved on, as if they had never broken the journey. Although Tuku couldn't see Mother's face in the dark, he could hear her breathing becoming louder and more erratic.

— *We should have been home hours ago*, she wailed. *We've always reached before nightfall, yes, before nightfall, Tuku. Where are they taking us? Oh Allah, what kind of creatures are they? They wouldn't let me see my mother; one last look, that's all I ask for.*

Mother sobbed for a while and then lapsed into a monotonous drone of prayer. Sulekha remained asleep on the floor and Tuku closed his side of the window. He leaned against the back plank, wrapped himself within the quilt, feeling so cosy. Now he imagined the slender legs of the palanquin bearers lashing against the dew-wet and tender thickets of grass. Perhaps they didn't notice that, perhaps they didn't even notice the thin moon marooned in the dark sky. But they seemed to have picked up their momentum even more. Yet they were so smooth, as if the palanquin wasn't moving at all. Only their soft, silky breaths waltzing with the light touches of their footfalls gave any impression of movement. He thought it was good that it was so dark, because Mother couldn't see his face. She couldn't see that there wasn't any sadness on his face any more. He was feeling so relaxed, in a strange way almost happy. Enveloped in the dark, and taken over completely by their music, he began to feel a secret complicity with the palanquin bearers. He wished that they would take him to a strange land, to a distant place. Even better, on a journey that would never end, but would go on for ever. That way he wouldn't have to arrive at Grandmother's home to see her dying, and he wouldn't have to say a final goodbye to the country. Yes, he was convinced that somehow the bearers understood his secret yearnings – the lonely whisper of his heart. Otherwise, why would the palanquin be moving like this through the night, along the paddy ridges and down meandering roads as if it didn't know how to stop? Surely, it was going towards a place beyond all known places, towards a place that he couldn't even imagine. Now he could hardly hear the bearers' breaths, as if they had attained a rare harmony with the air. Perhaps they did it because they were conscious of not wishing to disturb the passengers in the late hours of the night. Even the dogs had stopped panting. After all her prayers and sobbing for hours on end, Mother seemed to be exhausted; she was slumped in a stupor. Everything now seemed right for the palanquin to be gliding on its own like a dove's plume, shed from a tall, arching bamboo. And it did. At last Tuku could hear the insects of the night, chirping through the dark fissures of earth. He got up and slid open the window for a brief, final glance outside. There were the fireflies shooting up from the bushes and spinning and looping and gliding in the gleaming ecstasy of light. He closed the window, went back under the cosy warmth of his quilt and began dreaming of other journeys he would make. First he would take the four-thirty mail from Mymensingh to Soranpur, and then the palanquin, silently borne by the strange tall men with pale brown eyes and luxuriant moustaches. Sensing the approach of the palanquin from the wind, Grandmother would be hurrying across the inner courtyard, stooped over her short, twisted, snake-like stick. Smiling her toothless smile, and surrounded by her swans, she would never fail to peer out from the wattle fence and call his name. And it would always be at that precise moment when the sky would turn purple amidst a chorus of jackals.

# FRAGMENTS FROM THE LIFE OF THE NICEST MAN IN TOWN

Between rows of shops and jostles of hawkers on the pavement, it erupts in a flash, down Station Road, into an alleyway, innumerable feet blazing their way among a smoke of sand. At first only a few, but as they run, more and more join their ranks. Although they are not aware of it, they are all breathless, smelling blood and snorting. But they all know that it is only a matter of time before they catch up with him. In the midst of this eruption a blind beggar is almost trampled underfoot as he gropes for his coins, his begging bowl sent flying by the crowd. But he is less worried about himself than curious about what has created this commotion. He shouts, *Listen, honourable gentlemen, hello kind sirs, what's happening? Who are you chasing?* Someone from the crowd says, *Why so nosy, you blindy? Fancy a lynching or what? Who cares who it is; he got to be wicked as hell.*

This year the monsoon is long overdue. Many times tentative clouds have gathered low in the sky. Each time, people have looked up for drops of rain to cool their molten faces. But the clouds do not fall as rain, only disperse high above the horizon as if in a cruel alliance with the smog that draws a screen around the sun. It is murky and unbearably humid. Even under the

electric fan the lodger is sweating. He is sitting alone in a
newspaper office, waiting for the editor, who should have been
there hours ago. Seeing him sweating and somewhat nervous,
the peon offers him a tea or a sherbet. He is desperate for
something cool, but after a moment's hesitation he refuses. He
doesn't want to be seen with a cup or a glass on his lips when the
editor enters the room. He needs the job badly so he doesn't want
to do anything which might be seen as a breach of decorum. Now
that he is so close to the job, he doesn't want to take chances. He
goes to the window, looks down at the crowd below. Despite the
humidity, they are jostling and marching like soldier ants,
gathering food for the colony. They are oppressed by the heat,
but are prepared to do anything for some food. He sees children
in small groups, looking far younger than their ages, scouring the
pavements. Those who are lucky enough to be pressed into the
gangs of boot-polishers or assisting the eyeless and limbless
beggars can look forward to eating something decent. Others are
in hopeless competition with their deformed elders. He knows
what will happen because it always happens the same way.
Suddenly, one of them reaches a point when his hunger turns
him into a sleepwalker. After that it is all too predictable, his
hands go straight into one of those rows of food arranged on the
open stalls, and then flight. The lodger averts his eyes from the
crowd down below because he can't afford the nerves that may
leave him defenceless before the editor. He desperately wants
a cigarette. But it is out of the question now. He puts his hand
in his pocket and feels the tips and shreds of tobacco with his
sweaty fingers. Then the editor walks in without paying him any
attention. The lodger stands up to greet him. He remains
standing while the editor sinks in his seat and rummages a pile
of paper scattered on his desk. Still without looking at him the
editor lights a cigarette. When he looks up he blows smoke in the
lodger's face. *My dear fellow, you are in*, he says, *Go and find*

*the nicest man in town, you'll have a nice little story to begin with.*

The lodger can't believe his luck; he almost jumps with joy as he comes down the stairs. When he hits the street from the editor's office the peon comes rushing up behind him. The lodger knows what he wants. He takes out a five taka note and tosses it in the air. Before the peon can catch it, he turns around, and loses himself in the crowd.

He walks straight to the Salimar cafe for a tea. Not caring how much it will cost, he buys rounds for Salim and Altaf. He takes a sip leaning against the chair and lights a King Stork cigarette. Despite the humidity, he feels very light and almost cool. When Salim and Altaf pull his leg over his lucky break, he just blows his smoke, and smiles quietly to himself. He gives in quickly to their demands that they should be taken to a late-night movie. He will treat them to expensive seats in the lower circle.

Still feeling light, the lodger walks into the streets where the tar is melting in the heat and the crowd plods along, drenched in sweat and exhausted. Observing this the lodger begins to feel the heaviness of the humidity weighing on him. So he decides to get away from it all, and instead of going home, he crosses the railway line, and heads towards the outskirts of the town. He walks along the cracked mud road, past thickets of bamboo until he reaches the deserted country market. He stands under a peepal tree that gives a view of open countryside. He hopes to find the cool breeze that once lulled him to sleep on a similar day two summers back. But even the shade under the trees is inhospitable because there is no wind. He sees a bulbul bird gasping for air, its tongue protruding. Not a single leaf stirs. But his disappointment does not prevent him from thinking about his assignment: writing about the nicest man in town. He is so lucky, he thinks; the assignment couldn't be more simple. All he needs to do is go home and shadow his landlord for a few days

and take notes. Then it is simply a matter of writing them up and
he will have his first assignment done.

It does not take long for the lodger to get into the swing of his
new job; it comes almost naturally to him. From afar, crouching
behind a hedge, he sees Mia Mohossin walking away from the
promenading crowd. He follows him along the river bank, past
the dense beds of nettles and down the slope between the tall
tamarisks. Not many people come this way but Mia Mohossin,
unless it rains the whole day, never fails to walk there. Since the
lodger knows his landlord's routine, he carries on another
twenty paces or so along the bank, then sits under a krisnachura
tree and waits.

Mia Mohossin reaches the river bank through the tamarisks
and sits down in his usual place. He thinks he is alone but he still
looks around nervously to make sure that no one is around. Only
then does he start breaking open the monkey nuts with a flick of
his fingers and munching them with salt and pepper. He comes
here not to find his own thoughts but to lose himself in the flow
of the river. First, he places himself between the smooth curves
of the ripples rising and folding back on themselves to rise again,
and then follows the rainbow patchwork of the sails, gliding past
him. Sometimes, if he is lucky, he is blessed with the sight of
dolphins leaping in formation. No matter what troubles his
thoughts, these movements always calm him down. But today,
as for the last few days, the river seems to have come to a
standstill. Moreover, from where he is sitting, there is no more
than a narrow channel to see. What lies before him is the vast
expanse of bone-dry river bed.

Mia Mohossin's unease deepens at the sight of emaciated
men dragging their sand-packed bullock carts through the deep
grooves of sand on the river bed. Equally unnerving are the lines
of boatmen, straining doubled-up along the shore, towing their

heavily-laden cargo boats. Moreover, he can't get the lodger out
of his mind. Why has the damn fool been following him around?
Is he practising to be a policeman or what? He doesn't look the
type. Maybe the fellow's just keeping an eye on him for his wife.
Does she suspect he's keeping a woman on the side? Unlikely.
Perhaps she's making a big fuss about his safety. True, he has
been rather forgetful lately. But that, too, is most unlikely. Mia
Mohossin comes to the conclusion that the lodger must be a
pervert. What other reason could there be for his not leaving him
alone even when he is performing his private functions? Only
Allah knows what pleasure he gets out of it – or if he has some
more sinister motive. Mia Mohossin shudders. Perhaps he
should kick the lodger out, but then convinces himself that he
doesn't care as long as he pays his rent. Nonetheless, he curses
his luck for having such an imbecile as a lodger.

Predictably enough one page in the lodger's notebook is a
mere repetition of the previous one. Mia Mohossin is a man of
strict routine. As always he reaches the school well before the
caretaker unlocks the main gate and begins cluttering the
blackboard with mathematical formulas and abstruse solutions
as soon as he enters the classroom. But unlike the other teachers
in the school, he not only spares the boys the cane, but speaks
to them in a most kindly fashion. After school he goes to the
afternoon market to buy dried fish, and then to the riverside.
Along the way he receives salaams from groups of boys with a
slight nod of his forehead.

Feeling rather bored and hot, the lodger goes down the bank
and crosses the sandy bed to the channel of water. He tries to
cool his face with the water but the river is simmering beneath
its placid surface. He folds his trousers up to his knees, splashes
about aimlessly in the water, dreaming of cool melons and ice-
creams. Yes, it's a good idea to keep his new job a secret from

his landlord, at least until his first assignment is done. The
lodger laughs to himself, thinking what a fuss he'd make if he
told him, all fake modesty, how undeserving he is to be called
the nicest man in town. The lodger curses his luck for having to
follow such a worthless fellow. He's sure that he gets a kick when
people call him the nicest man in town. He'd rather call him
damn stupid, because his landlord doesn't know that people
laugh behind his back. OK, he gets his salaam but the lodger is
convinced that this is simply out of habit. But the old fool loves
it. He's laughable really, the lodger thinks, playing the saint at
a time like this – the only incorruptible soul in town. What a
lousy feat. Let's see how long the marathon man can run, the
lodger tells himself. God he's so boring, so utterly boring.

Yet, the lodger is sure that he noticed something rather more
interesting about the town's nicest man in the market the day
before. Mia Mohossin, as always in the afternoon, was there to
buy his dried fish. But didn't he, while edging between the
jostling crowd, eye the goat's meat hanging from the butcher's
shop with a certain greediness, not to say lust? Further on from
the butcher's shop, Mia Mohossin paused, yes he paused by the
chemist's shop to look at the aftershave lotions in the window.
Perhaps he was envious of those of his colleagues who shaved
regularly and came to school with *Brut* or *Old Spice* on their
faces. Everybody knew that they could purchase such luxuries
only with immoral earnings. But unlike that bloody lot, Mia
Mohossin wouldn't make a corrupt business deal with those ex-
students who had reached high official rank. Nor would he sell
himself to the government party for promotion. He seemed
contented to be poor and good. Yet the lodger saw something
different when Mia Mohossin looked at the goat meat and the
aftershave lotions in the window.

When the lodger returns from the water to the bank, he sees
that the crimson of the sky has already given way to purple. Soon

it will be grey and then darkness will fall. But the heat is still percolating through all living bodies with the same intensity.

Now that it is time to go home, Mia Mohossin once more looks around nervously, buttons his shirt up to his neck, kicks the nut shells down the slope, and emerges from behind the tamarisk bushes. He takes the short cut home across the playing field.

The lodger follows him, as always circumspectly.

There is a puny little boy, shrunk far below his age, running down the alleyway. Chasing him is a crowd, wild with the prospect of a kill. Most of them are silent expect for their grunts and heavy breathing. But small groups from different parts of the crowd are shouting at the tops of their voices. If one of the groups is shouting, *There goes a thief*, another cries, *A pickpocket*, another, *A vicious dacoit*. But they are all shouting, *Get him, get that pig's litter, oh honest folks, get that motherfucker.*
  – *So, brothers, what did he do?*
  – *What a stupid question. Are you one of them thieves or what? Just look at him: evil is written all over him, isn't it? Look, mister, look carefully, don't you see how his spare ribs stick out, his eyes pop out, his cheeks are hollowed in, his belly swollen like a balloon. He's got to be evil, the devil himself – no?*

Mia Mohossin sits on the veranda, chews paan leaves, and smokes his hookah. Rather hesitantly, the lodger comes in, bids him salaam, and sits on the stairs to the veranda. Both of them remain silent until Mia Mohossin, between puffs of his hookah, says:
  – *You look a trifle overworked, my boy. What have you been up to?*
  – *Nothing sir, just went to town to buy a few things.*

– *Is that so. Seen anything interesting?*

– *The usual things, Sir. Oh, I'd almost forgotten, there has been another mass beating, Sir.*

– *I see.*

– *A boy, Sir. About eight or nine. He was a goner, Sir, right there, in front of me.*

– *What did you do, my boy? Enjoyed a good look, eh?*

– *I had good reasons, Sir.*

– *Of course, my boy, you had good reasons.*

– *If you were there, sir, what would you have done?*

– *But I wasn't there, was I? Anyway, you should have been by the riverside. You know, things were much more interesting up there.*

After that brief exchange, they are silent again. Mia Mohossin leans back in his easy chair, puffs away on his hookah, water bubbling inside. The lodger gets up quietly, goes to his room and puffs his King Storks nervously. Once again night comes, windless, humid, mosquitoes running wild on human flesh. But still there is no rain. Nobody can sleep in a night like this. Only those who have been overcome by exhaustion have closed their eyes.

About nine at night Mia Mohossin's wife comes to the veranda to announce supper. Mia Mohossin, his wife and the lodger sit down on the floor to eat, under a dim light. They are all sweating profusely. Nobody says a word until the lodger says that the boy was hungry, terribly hungry. Mia Mohossin pretends not to have heard, but the wife leaps up at the news.

– *Who have they killed this time?* says the wife, suspending her fingers halfway to her mouth.

– *A bad character of some sort, but I'm not sure,* says the lodger.

– *Who are the good characters then? Have you seen any lately, my boy?* says the wife.

*— What are you talking about, Aunty? There must be some good people around,* answers the lodger hesitantly, looking at Mia Mohossin.

*— Ah, the nincompoops, the shitting types; they are only pure by default, my boy,* says the wife.

*— What do you mean?* asks the lodger.

*— Why! those spineless ones, of course, who wet their pants when the main chance comes, my boy. You see them going around stroking their scrotum-length beards, pretending to be goody-goody types*, answers the wife before resuming the delicate movement of hand to mouth.

During the whole conversation Mia Mohossin remains aloof but he eats his rice at a furious pace. Of course, the lodger hasn't failed to notice this. He smiles nervously, licks his fingers, tasting the chilli-heat and dried fish. He is thinking: So the good ones are good-for-nothing types – oh, what an amusing state of affairs.

Mia Mohossin is rocking on the veranda, closing his eyes as if trying to pick up any sign of the imminent wind in a distant rustles of leaves. He has resigned himself to wait for sleep until the small hours when the earth will be cool enough. Some of the neighbouring children are reading loudly, rhythmically, repeating, memorising, defying the twin assaults of humidity and mosquitoes. Outside, restless youths are roaming the streets and eyeing the girls, silhouetted behind thick curtains. After a while his wife comes to the veranda to say that she is going to bed. Mia Mohossin follows her, rubs coconut oil on her head and fans the palm-leaf fan until she falls asleep. While he is inside, the lodger comes to sit on the veranda. Mia Mohossin can't sleep, so he comes back to the veranda again. Seeing him, the lodger hurriedly stubs out his King Stork, unleans his back from the wooden pole and sits up straight, rubbing his neck. Mia Mohossin leans back in his easy chair, blows on his chillum to revive the charcoal balls, but they seem dead. Before Mia Mohossin can get up to look for the matches, the lodger springs to his feet to help; he blows with all of his lungs, scattering ashes on his face. When he sees the embers flicker on the charcoal balls, burning the tobacco, he goes back to sit on the same spot. Not looking at each other, they remain silent for a while until Mia Mohossin clears his throat with a cough and asks:

— *Have you heard the strange parable of the king and the rain water, my boy ?*

— *Yes, sir, I have heard of it. Didn't the rain water contain the seed of madness?*

— *Yes, my boy, all the subjects in the kingdom took that water except, of course, the king and his chief minister.*

— *So the king and his chief minister remained the only sane characters in the kingdom of madness.*

— *Exactly. Now, remember, what happened to the king and his chief minister, my boy?*

— *When all the mad subjects saw the king and his chief minister in the darbar administering justice with their customary seriousness they began to laugh at them. They thought the king and the chief minister were utterly mad.*

— *Then?*

— *The king and the chief minister drank the same rain water that his clever chief minister had saved up and went mad themselves. Obviously, to stay sane in the eyes of their subjects.*

— *What a terrible story, don't you agree, my boy?*

— *Yes, sir, but who could deny its truthfulness, specially at a time like this.*

— *So you think we are bound to repeat the parable once more.*

— *If I may be so impertinent to say, none of us is immune, Sir. Of course, there are always rare exceptions. Some wouldn't touch that rain water for anything.*

*– But you think that the exception is a fable, don't you, my boy?*

The last question catches the lodger off his guard; he is searching his mind to say something in response. But Mia Mohossin is not waiting to hear him any more. He has already begun puffing his hookah, rocking his chair and going deeper into his thoughts. So the lodger doesn't dare to open his mouth again. He gets up quietly and says good night to Mia Mohossin and goes back to his room.

Hours go by. Mia Mohossin chews paan leaves, puffs his hookah and finally, well past midnight, leaves the veranda. He goes to the small shed next to the chicken-coop where he has a table at which he writes in his diary before going to sleep.

Lying face up in his bed in the dark, but with ears as alert as ever, and nervously smoking his King Storks, the lodger senses every movement that Mia Mohossin is making. He hears Mia Mohossin leave the shed and go to his bedroom, then he waits patiently for a while to make sure that Mia Mohossin is asleep. Only then does he tiptoe to the shed. He is not used to its layout, so he disturbs a hen, which cackles; he freezes for a few long seconds. Fortunately, the hen soon calms down and he opens the diary under the dim light of a torch. Under today's entry Mia Mohossin has simply written: *I had a terrible urge to beat the hell out of my boys today*. Reading that the lodger smiles to himself, thinking that Mia Mohossin is cracking up. Well, what do you know! The assignment could be quite interesting after all.

In the morning, as usual, Mia Mohossin leaves home at 8 o' clock sharp, and goes to school. Around midday, thunder rips the murky sky but there is still no rain. Inside the classroom, the boys are sweating. Their minds are not on their lessons, they are poking each other with the nibs of their pens and pencils. Some one on the back row is masturbating and others are screaming at the punkha-puller to pull his punkha faster and faster. Already drenched in sweat, and exhausted, the punkha-puller pulls his punkha frantically until he collapses, his whole substance spent. Oblivious to his plight, the boys demand his immediate ejection; they are now throwing paper planes at Mia Mohossin. As soon as the bell rings, the boys jostle one another as they rush out, almost knocking Mia Mohossin down. They trample over the skeletal body of the punkha-puller, run across the playing field and jump into the pond to cool themselves. Mia Mohossin sprinkles water on the punkha-puller's face but he doesn't come around. He goes to the Head to report. The Head says, *Leave the lazy-good-for-nothing where he is; the rascal is only pretending*. He comes back to the punkha-puller, pours more water over his face; still he doesn't come round. Mia Mohossin is sure that the punkha-puller is dead. But he loses his nerves when he sees the menacing figure of the Head approaching down the corridor. He leaves the punkha-puller and rushes out of the school.

It is afternoon. The terrible humidity is rising and rising and the sky is getting murkier. Soon it will rain. But how to pass the time until then. Mia Mohossin walks to the market with his umbrella under his arm. People are too busy sustaining themselves until the rain comes to greet him with their customary salaams. But the lodger is there following him as soon as he takes the asphalt road at the end of the footpath from the school. Melon-wallahs, ice-wallahs, sherbet-wallahs are doing good business. How nice a glass of sherbet with ice would be. And why not? Mia Mohossin pinches a taka from the shopping money and cools himself with a papaya sherbet. He gets extra ice – *Sir, it's special for you*, says the sherbet-wallah. He hasn't gone far down the road before the smouldering heat dries him up again. Despite being worn-out, the rickshaw-pullers do not stop, they are peddling away with their withered legs, carrying threes and fours up and down the road, racing against each other in a frantic peal of bells. Mia Mohossin goes down College Road, past the pink municipal building, turns the corner of Little Market Road, and reaches Station Road. God knows what mad fancy takes him; he is out to blow his shopping money. He enters a barber's shop with an electric fan and high-cushioned chairs. He goes in for a shave and asks for *Old Spice* at the end. It nearly empties his pocket. It's worth it, yes, it's worth it; it cools his face. He has to look after himself a bit for a change. *Yes, give me a massage, the full treatment.*

Now everybody is joining in, swelling the crowd, chasing the boy into an alleyway that leads to a cul-de-sac. With nowhere else to go, the boy runs blindly to the wall, scratching his fingernails on it as he tries to climb it, but it's no use. He still doesn't get rid of the piece of bread though, but stuffs it in his mouth, turns around, chewing the bread, and waits for the crowd to get him. Seeing the boy motionless, the crowd pauses a second or two. Then a group breaks away towards the boy. Abruptly the barber removes the cape off Mia Mohossin as he rushes to join the crowd; Mia Mohossin follows him. Already they have knocked the boy down. Now some of them are kicking him, while others pull his hair. Another group jumps on the boy with bricks in their hands; they break his joints. Blood trickles through his mouth. He is quiet, not crying or pleading for mercy, but still eating the piece of bread. Someone says, *Look, how wicked he is, he is still eating, the son-of-a-bitch is enjoying it. So brother, just for a piece of bread? Always making excuses for the wicked, they are always getting away, but this one is not going anywhere. We got him.* Finally the sky breaks – odd drops of rain are falling on the ground and evaporating in the heat. Mia Mohossin pushes through the crowd and finds just enough of a gap to slip through his umbrella. He is poking the boy with its sharp metallic point, he is searching for a soft patch, and finally finding the right spot, he bores it into the boy's body. A fat guy, with an enormous erection under his lungi, hurls himself onto the boy's throat and squeezes the life out of him. The last piece of bread, the brown crusty bit he just couldn't finish in time, lies on the boy's protruding tongue. Now the rain is pouring down. Mia Mohossin wipes the metallic end of his umbrella in a tussock of grass. He does not unfurl his umbrella. Nor does the lodger. It will now rain for days, for the monsoon is here.

Mia Mohossin changes his clothes, sits in his rocking chair and begins to smoke his hookah. His wife asks him about the shopping. Mia Mohossin tells her, *Silly me, how careless of me, I have been pickpocketed; ask the lodger, he has seen it all*. The wife doesn't make any fuss because she believes his story. She borrows some rice from a neighbour and cooks khichuri. Mia Mohossin eats with such a passion, licking his fingers, breaking green chillies with each mouthful, chewing loudly, belching as if he is about to reach orgasm. Even his wife is baffled. *Is the khichuri that good or are you just hungry in a big big way? Maybe you're just getting greedier in your old age*. Mia Mohossin doesn't look up to answer his wife; he is totally lost in his eating. After the meal, the same routine: the rocking chair, chewing tobacco leaves, smoking the hookah, and writing his diary before going to sleep. As he has been doing for the last few days, the lodger too goes to the shed to read the diary, with his customary circumspection. But he knows that it is the last time because his search has ended. Luckily the hen in the coop stays quiet. He opens Mia Mohossin's diary with quivering excitement. How would he reflect on what has happened that day? Mia Mohossin has written: *Finally it is raining; the khichuri was delicious – the best I've tasted for a long time; my good wife hasn't yet lost her touch. Goodbye, my young friend, your company has been a delightful experience*. The lodger feels at a loss at the casualness of Mia Mohossin's attitude. Why hasn't he reflected at all, let alone shown any remorse over what has happened. God, the way the bugger enjoyed his khichuri! Anyway, what's the meaning of saying goodbye to me, what game is he playing?

Late in the night, the lodger is sitting at his desk, sucking his teeth, smoking a King Stork. In front of him, between piles of books and paper-cuttings, lies his notebook, its remaining yellowish, brittle pages waiting to be filled with black ink. King-size rain drops are bouncing off the tin roof; coconut trees are swaying, their long fronds swinging frantically and whistling through the cool night. The overhanging mango branches dip their succulent green leaves to lash against the corrugated roof. Gurgling water rushes through the dried-up drains. Everyone is curled up in their beds, catching up on the sleep lost in the humidity of the past few days. Nobody will venture out on a night like this. The lodger shakes his fountain pen, scattering ink on the floor. He writes, *I am sure the man with the umbrella was Mia Mohossin, although among the jostling bodies converging on the boy, it wasn't possible to pick up each face distinctly.* Suddenly lightning flashes across the sky, revealing the ceaseless stream beyond the window pane. *I was there, perched on a high wall, watching the scene as if at the cinema or as if I was a photo journalist looking through the lens, detached, simply recording an event. My subject was Mia Mohossin; the scene is incomplete without him, he had to be there, just like everybody else.* It will rain the whole night and for weeks on end. *Suppose the boy was to return to point his finger at the guilty?* The lodger laughs smugly, lighting a King Stork and turning over a page, writing. *Yes, let him come back, at least for one last time.* A gust of wind rattles the window latch, rustling the paper-cuttings. Though he doesn't hear him enter through the main gate, cross the water-logged vegetable patch and step onto the veranda, the lodger senses his presence as he opens the front door to slip into the house. The black ink has already smeared the last page of the notebook. He's quite certain that he's there now, the footfalls distinct as he unlocks the doors. He is going straight down the long arm of this L-shaped house towards the third room where Mia Mohossin is sleeping beside his wife. He is sure he is going for him; the bugger deserves it. But before he reaches Mia Mohossin's room, the slapping sound of two tiny wet feet on the bare floor stops, pauses for some indecisive seconds, then starts again, getting louder. He is coming back, coming towards the front of the house and turning right to where the lodger is writing his notebook. He is looking for the eyes that watched, as if through a camera lens, the death of a boy in which everybody participated except him.

# THE MAPMAKERS OF SPITALFIELDS

It was Friday afternoon and we were at the Sonar Bangla cafe. There was a long queue, but that didn't surprise us. It was always jam-packed at this time of the week with regulars looking for a moment's respite from the toils and traumas of the week. Between gossiping about the playback song numbers and the dance routines in the latest videos, and between humdrum news from faraway home and savouring the spicy delicacies on offer, they drifted into another world. We sat squashed in a corner, under a painting of a boat coming straight down from the horizon, where the sun has just risen above a hazy line of trees. Badal was trying desperately to break through the cacophony of noise and catch the oarsman's song blaring from the loud-speaker at the far end of the cafe. Shafique, in between spoonfuls of halva, was glancing furtively at a gourd which was protruding from his knitted jute shopping bag. I was leaning against the chair to fork a piece of kebab. At that moment, the front door flung open and two blond men in white overalls came following the cold wind which galloped through the length of the cafe. Sensing danger, everyone ducked into their shells, except the oarsman, who went on singing until he scaled down from the breathless heights he had climbed. Jaws tight, the two paced the whole length of the floor in their purposeful red doc-martens, looking for someone or something out of the corners of their eyes.

Abruptly, they stopped behind a man wearing a flannel suit and a broad brimmed hat, then went to the front of him to scrutinise his face. They shook their heads as they walked towards us. They leant over our table, inscrutable, except for a knowing twist of their lips, saying nothing, but like well-trained bloodhounds trying to sniff out an odour of a clue. We knew their game, so we too kept our mouths shut. Seeing that we hadn't lost our nerves, the smoother of the two produced a photo from his pocket and laid it on the table. While he questioned us with the utmost politeness, his companion stood impassive in his towering bulk. When he saw that his smooth companion wasn't getting anywhere, he lifted his heavy eyelids, giving us a menacingly inquisitive look with his pale blue eyes. We shook our heads and said we hadn't seen the man in the photograph before. Nor had anyone else in the cafe. The bloodhounds didn't look very pleased. Mr Smooth lost his cool. He screwed up his eyebrows and thumped the table. Mr Nasty thrust his bulk forward to redouble his menace.

– *It's too bad, mate*, said Smooth, *the whole business stinks. I know the game you're playing, but it sickens me, really it does. How far would you go to protect your own kind, eh? For God's sake, the geezer's a lunatic. An absolute nutter, you know. Have you ever seen the way he walks, have you, huh? We can't let him roam the street like that, you know. We want to take him in for his own good.*

We still kept our mouths shut. Suddenly becoming thoughtful, as if he had hit upon something, Smooth paused to scrutinise my face.

– *What they call you?*

I gave him my name.

– *Don't play games with me, mate. You know what I mean. What they call you around here?*

I again repeated my name. He snapped the photo off the table and they left together as hastily as they had come.

For quite some time after they left, the silence wasn't broken, until someone nervously struck a match and many of the regulars reached for their cigarettes. We didn't want to hang around, so before the other customers could emerge from their shells and break into a cacophony of feverish questions and improbable answers, we hit the street. It was only four in the afternoon but already getting dark. We looked in both directions to make sure the guys in white overalls weren't around and headed east along Hanbury Street. We walked briskly in the cold. Shafique, as he always did when nervous, whistled out of tune. Badal, between puffs of his cigarette, looked thoughtful. But I knew he was dying to ask me about Brothero-Man. We didn't talk as we walked on, but I shuddered at the thought of the two men in white overalls catching up with Brothero-Man. When we were passing Spelman Street I thought I saw a silhouetted figure emerge from an alleyway and disappear into the maze of high-rise flats. Was that Brothero-Man? But I wasn't so anxious for him now because I knew they wouldn't be able to catch him at this hour. He had this thing about twilight and dawn. Each day, at those uncertain moments between day and night, he applied himself most skilfully. Not only did he outflank their hesitations with the supreme subtleties of his craft, but went onto a different plane altogether. Now that it was twilight they would be lucky to catch even a faint glimpse of his shadow. Yet, he never hurried, always laid one foot in front of the other with the utmost precision as he went back and forth, sketching delicately, with the skill of a miniaturist, a map at the very heart of this foreign city.

We walked together as far as Commercial Street. Finally Badal's nerves got the better of him; and just before we parted, he asked me:

*– He isn't really mad, is he?*

I almost said – *Why do you ask me? How should I know?* – but I didn't say anything. Anyway, he didn't push me for an answer. Badal and Shafique said goodbye and went towards Whitechapel Station. I came back the way we had come. I wanted to find Brothero-Man and warn him about the mad-catchers in white overalls.

Soon I found myself at the side of the high-rise complex that lines the middle section of Hanbury Street. When I looked up I saw the faint outlines of saris and lungis, festooned, fluttering from the washing lines. I couldn't help laughing, because they looked as dashing at the task of flying the flag as the Union Jack had done in the olden days. Suddenly I saw some garment, cut loose by a gust of wind, floating like a kite. I watched it disappear into the darkness. Even before I reached the concrete play-ground in front of the tower blocks, I could smell burning spices escaping through crevices in doorways and windows. Within, the whole building oozed spices, an aromatic aura which made it seem like a secret zone in another country. I could have closed my eyes and still reached the tower blocks by following the trails laid by the spices. Looking at the clothes hanging on the parapet I thought of Brothero-Man and his meticulousness for colours. For instance, if white was the chosen colour of the day, then the obligatory white flannel suit would be matched by immaculately polished white shoes and a white broad-brimmed felt hat. The only contrast, apart from his own skin, would be added by a violet tie. Then he would be ready to walk the streets like a tip-top man. Irrespective of the season and the weather, he came this way every day, and more than once, to look at the washing lines, to breathe in the burning spices, and laugh, baring his gold teeth. Nights had their own routines, but in the day he would sit on the parapet, watching the children playing games and singing rhymes. How he loved the rhymes – oh what sweet rhymes they were. Those Bengali ones, learnt from the hums and lullabies of their mothers, were mixing with the *hickory dickory dock* of those English ones. At first the children used to throw stones at him, pull his jacket from behind and scream at him, *Mad mad mad, there goes a stark-pagal-mad, who is madder than the hatter-mad*. But soon they came to accept him as a permanent landmark in their playground, like the parapet on which he sat. Mind you, unlike the parapet, Brothero-Man had bottomless pockets, bulging with goodies beyond the children's wildest dreams. When they were most absorbed in their games, Brothero-Man would tilt his broad-brimmed felt hat over his face, pretending to have fallen asleep. But the children knew it to be the signal for a more enchanting game and they would come rushing towards him. Seeing the children out of the corner of his eye, he would push the broad brim to the back of his head and say, *Little brotheros and little sisteros, abracadabra, are you ready for Alibaba's magic-jadu show?* Then he would conjure up, with a deft play of his fingers, the latest models of toys, expensive sweets, and even puppies and kittens from the bottoms of his pockets. He would hand them in to the boys and girls with a grin on his face. Ah, he was happy then – my brothero.

Before I could emerge from the depths of thought that Brothero-Man always demanded of me, I had already crossed the poorly-lit playground, and was facing the lift. It, as usual, wasn't working. So I took the stairs to the 7th floor. It didn't bother me much because I was used to walking. Munir opened the door. I asked him if he had seen Brothero-Man. He hadn't seen him around lately. Overhearing us, Soraya came rushing from the kitchen. Yes, she had seen him that very afternoon on his usual spot on the parapet, watching the children play. As usual every Friday, the theme of the day was yellow. But it was a new outfit, Soraya told me, and how handsome he looked in it. Before I could ask about little Tariq, he was already next to me, but sensing the serious tone of our conversation, he stood silent. I was rubbing his head but not paying him any attention. A bit offended, he tugged at my jacket, looked at me with his huge dark eyes and asked if I had any sweets for him. I rummaged my pockets but found nothing. He pulled a face, went to his mother and stood staring sadly at the floor, holding onto the edge of her sari. When I promised that I would take him to see giraffes tomorrow, he looked happy. He smiled saying *loooong neck* – and went back inside.

Soraya offered to make me a tea. When I said no, she asked if I would try some rice bread she had already made. I declined this too, saying I was in a hurry. She looked concerned, but didn't ask me any further questions. I had taken my leave and was almost out of the door when Munir asked me why I was looking for Brothero-Man. I told him about the guys in white overalls. Knowing Munir well, I didn't expect him to be sympathetic but I was surprised when I heard him say:

– *You know, it wouldn't be a bad idea if he goes in for a while. Let's face it, the guy's utterly mad. Look at the funny way he dresses. My God – the colours! Tell me something, how can a sane person walk about all day so aimlessly? And where does he go? Absolutely nowhere. And his talk, God, the amount of rubbish he talks. Honestly, I can't make any sense of his babbles; I'm not even sure whether he speaks Bengali or English. You might not agree, but I think he needs treatment. The people you saw in white overalls must be professionals. We've no reason to be worried about them. I'm sure they came only to help.*

Soraya bit her lips with bitterness, as if something had finally snapped between herself and Munir.

– *I can't believe I'm hearing these things from you, Munir. What's happened to you? Have you eaten your head or what? I thought at least you'd be able to tell the difference between a mad man and a wise man. Have you bothered to listen to him? If you had, I'm sure you wouldn't say these things. Oh Allah, what nonsense I'm hearing! You think him a funny-ike because he dares to speak the truth like the prophets.*

I was saddened by the widening gulf between them. But what could I do? So I left them to their arguments and once more took to Hanbury Street.

The Sonar Bangla was buzzing again with regulars. Even from outside I could hear the oarsman's song. A lonely shore had no doubt prompted him into full flight, dared him to climb an unattainable scale. I walked past quickly, slipped across the road and went into the youth club. There the wacko guy Jacko ruled the scene like an absolute monarch from the jukebox, funking BAD BAD beats. All around the joint, Bengali youths, all them styling in cool leather jackets, hung around hyped on black-Afro-man's vibes. Between quick shuffles of their feet, they cued on the green tables, and crossed over to the other side. Where did they go? Harlem, Kingston, or just Brixton down the road? It didn't matter to Brothero-Man. God, how he loved the place. If you could fathom his mumble, you would have heard him saying, *Goodly goodly delectation, look-look, dhekho-dhekho, such a first-class scene.*

From where they got the knack, nobody knew, but these youths had mastered martial arts to the black belt class. And kick for kick they faced the skin-headed boys in uni-jacks. Brothero-Man had a real thing for the boys. He once told me, *Brothero, do you hear what them farty-wurty mouths say? Them say how the boys have gone kaput – neither here nor there – lost in the shit-hole of a gulla-zero. What a fucking-wukking talk that is, brothero. What do you say, eh? Laugh, brothero, laugh. Sure, them don't got the brain, even the goat shit size. Aren't they everywhere, brothero, aren't these boys everywhere? Hey brothero, you're looking at tiring miring biring the king Brick Lane piring.* When the boys at the club heard Brothero-Man talk like that, they would laugh. *What the fuck you're on, Brothero-Man? We don't dig you right.* Sure, the boys at the club thought him a bit crazy, but they had a soft spot for him too. When Asad saw me from the table, he hurried with his shot and came over.

– *What's up?*

I told him about the guys in white overalls. He went quiet, shook his head.

– *I tell you something: the fuckers are playing with fire. If they touch him, things will burn. And they'll have a riot on their hands.*

He went back to his table and blasted the cue into the pack, scattering the red and the yellow balls in disorder across the green baize.

Surfacing from the youth club I continued ahead, around the corner into Brick Lane. Suddenly I felt the cold like an icy syringe digging deep under my skin. But I had to keep looking. I put my hands, bluish from the cold, into my pockets, flung the long scarf over my head and walked on. Along the way I remembered the first time I met Brothero-Man. How long ago was beside the point, but it was memorable for being one of those rare sunny days in winter. I remember waking that morning, opening the window and letting the soft sunlight drape me with the fragility of muslin. Unwisely, I put on only a light jacket and almost in a dream set off down the Brick Lane way. Before I could get my bearings, Brothero-Man had already leapt on me from nowhere on the springs of his legs. *Good morning-salaam. Welcome, brothero, how do you do-doo, brothero?* I must have had looked at him with puzzlement, if not with fear, but even then I could sense that he was a brother. Almost immediately, before I could reply, he had left me, though he paused a second to look back and smiled at me showing a glint of his golden teeth. I looked on as he, apparently untouched by the cold, melted into an alleyway. Later, much later, I learned that he had been walking these streets for the last twenty years. Before that, nothing was certain. But few doubted the rumour that he was a shareng on a ship from the Indies. He must have been one of the pioneer jumping-ship men, who landed in the East End and lived by bending the English tongue to the umpteenth degree.

There are many who date the day he took to walking as the beginning of his madness. But others mark it as the beginning of that other walk when, patiently, and bit by bit, he began drawing the secret blueprint of a new city. It wasn't exactly in the likeness of our left-behind cities from the blossoms of memories. Nor did it grow entirely from the soon-to-be razed foreign cities where we travellers arrived with expectant maps in our dreams. What do you say, brothero? Surely a strange new city, always at the crossroads, and between the cities of lost times and cities of times yet to come.

I was still walking along Brick Lane and entered once more the zone of spices. But this time their scents tempting from the rows of restaurants were overlaid with gentle aromas from the sweet shops and smells of leather from the sweat shops. Ambling towards Aldgate East station, I paused to look at the mannequins in a brightly-lit sari shop, their plumpish bodies wrapped in the latest styles of silk, cotton and synthetic saris. I knew that Brothero-Man would have lingered here with his eyes fixed on the mannequins. Then he would have taken his hat off to comb his hair in the reflection of the window. Often, when the shop was open, he would go inside and run his fingers along the rows of saris. It would please him to see the fluttering colours and hear secret melodies in the rustles of silk. Sensing Brothero-Man's presence, the owner of the shop, Zamshed Mia – who never usually spent an idle moment not making a profit – would look up at the spy monitor and stay there rapt for minutes on end. These moments never failed to bring tears to his eyes because he'd never seen so much tenderness in a man's caress before.

Desperate to repay him in some way, but not knowing what to do, one day he offered Brothero-Man one of his most expensive saris. He told him that perhaps he could send it to his beloved. Brothero-Man flung the sari in his face and told him that his beloveds were right there in the shop window. After that he gave Zamshed Mia the full treatment of his foul mouth. Zamshed Mia didn't understand exactly what he meant; such mysteries, he thought, were beyond him. From then on he would only look in silence at the miracle of love in the black and white video monitor. I wondered what topographical details the map-maker had been noting here, and moved on.

Not far from here was a popular newsagent, selling imported books, magazines from Bangladesh, and Bollywood videos. I entered the shop, picked up a copy of the weekly *Natun Din* and went up to pay Kamal at the counter. I asked him if he had seen Brothero-Man. Of course, he had been there in the morning, as he always was, ever since the shop opened. He'd browsed through the latest magazines, Kamal said, and asked for his favourite songs to be put on. He seemed his usual happy self, but while reading a news item he had gone quiet and muttered to himself in his fucking-wucking, obscene language. Kamal told me, too, that two guys in white overalls had also recently been in his shop, asking questions about Brothero-Man. They'd told him that they would hunt him the whole night. Whatever it took, they wouldn't leave without him.

– *He's a bit funny-like, I admit*, Kamal said. *But my old man thinks he got some kinda special power. He sees some deep meaning in his walk. I don't dig all that, but he's harmless, ain't he?'*

I was once more on Brick Lane, walking its littered pavements. Night had fallen some hours ago and even the groceries with incredibly long hours were closing. But the flutter of cab lights would go on for the whole stretch of the night, and the restaurants and pubs still had a few profitable hours left to run. I wondered why the guys in white overalls were so desperate to catch Brothero-Man before the end of the night. Perhaps they'd got wind of his secret map-making. Yes, but why couldn't they wait any longer than this night? Then it occurred that perhaps they had a hunch that he was on the last leg of his survey, and one more night would complete the map. Surely, they would do anything in their powers to prevent that.

I felt a renewed urgency to find Brothero-Man before the guys in white overalls. I was moving briskly when I saw one of the regular tramps of the lane, soaked in alcohol, emerging from a dark recess. He staggered towards me, rubbed his mouth with his trembling hand and strained his half-closed eyes as if trying to tell who it was. But his drunkenness and the darkness of the Lane prevented him from recognising me.

—*I'll let you in on a secret, Guv. You're looking at the real Jack the Ripper. How about it? Give me a fag, will ya?*

I didn't have any cigarettes, so instead I put a twenty pence piece in his hand. He looked well pleased. I left him and headed towards the Haji Shahab's grocery. It was closed but the lights were on. Through the glass front I saw the Haji counting what looked like a lot of money. The takings must have been good because he had a grin on his paan-red lips. When I knocked on the glass door, I saw panic in the Haji's eyes. He dropped the money in the till and slammed it shut. He looked around, holding onto his long hennaed beard until he saw me. Only then did he look relieved and the grin came back to his lips. He opened the door and bid me a warm salaam. He locked the door behind us and offered me a cigarette. Twirling his beard he said:

— *Where is your friend, country brother? What's his name — the one who calls everyone brothero? I tell you something, no one looks at my fish like him. Only Allah knows why he looks that way. But I'm sure they aren't ordinary looks. What do you say, country brother?* I said I hadn't seen him for the last few days and was looking for him desperately. The Haji said that Brothero-Man had been there that morning, as ever devouring his fishes with his eyes. It was one of his rendezvous – a necessary stop in his walking routine. The last time I'd come, I remembered, I was with him. Together we'd stood in contemplative silence looking at the fishes. We were so absorbed that at first we didn't notice the Haji standing just behind us, rubbing his portly belly. We were somewhat startled when he spoke.

*– Oh, what do you say, country brothers? They're as desirable as hourries, eh? If you gobble them up like this, with your hungry eyes, my customers will get bad stomach, no?*

Brothero-Man looked at him fiercely and gritted his gold teeth.

*– Look at him, brothero, look what a nasty piece of fussing-wussing gob. I'm telling you, brothero, he was sure raised on hog-shit. Look, how he hides his wickedness under his beard. And his portly sack, look at it, how it hangs over his nasty thing. Who knows, brothero, how many bastards he raised with that thing. Sure, him's as greedy as a shit-eating-hog. Always fussing-wussing, I tell you, brothero, him eating too much rice. Hish, mish, bish, I'm the king kish.*

I had never seen the Haji looking so scared because he couldn't quite decide whether Brothero-Man was a mad man or a holy man. In his confusion he offered Brothero-Man a cigarette. He took it, lit it and stormed out. Much later, he told me that the Haji had his own value because, like the fishes, he was good to look at.

I told the Haji about the two men in white overalls. He shook his head and said that they would make a grave mistake if they touched him, because only Allah knew what would happen to them.

*– I wouldn't be surprised, if they were ruined for generations, country brother.*

I was back on the street and once more I was walking along Brick Lane. When I was passing the mosque I couldn't help but stop, because Brothero-Man would have stopped here. Of course, I didn't go in, because he never went in. Almost like clockwork he comes five times a day and stands outside. He stares at the gloomy facade of the mosque and chats with the regulars who go in for prayers. Once, one of these asked him why he never went inside the mosque. He paid dearly for asking that silly question because Brothero-Man was in good form that day.

*— Inside/Outside what a fussing-wussing talk. Have you any idea, you shit head, where that mosque be? Right in me inside. Well, well, now tell me, you mother-fucking donkey, how can I go inside of the inside? Bawkk, bawk, bawk not knowing how to talk.*

It was late and the last prayer of the day had been said some hours ago. I stood in the cold wind that blew across the Lane and looked at the Mosque. It was still full of his presence. He was there, my brothero, always there.

Where could I go from the mosque? Oh yes, I could always go and see my friend the poet who lived across the road. So I crossed the road and walked ahead and within seconds I was outside his door. I pressed the button and waited. Suddenly I saw a blue van braking abruptly and skidding a little on the icy road. Out came the two guys in white overalls, walking slowly towards Commercial Street. Did they have a lead on Brothero-Man? I knew that they'd never find the pathways through the secret grids of his map. But if Brothero-Man — for some strange reason — wanted to be found?

My friend the poet opened the door. I climbed the dark stairs behind his rumbling bulk and ancient odour. He once told me, between a roaring laugh and dropping ash from his cigarette, that he cultivated that stink as a protection against his enemies. We all laughed but there was some truth in it. If you weren't seasoned in his friendship you would puke the moment you went anywhere near him. But now the stink made me forget, at least for a brief moment, about Brothero-Man. Back in his room, the poet resumed his reclining posture on the divan and lit a cigarette. Closing his eyes, he blew smoke into air already densely clouded with smoke from hundreds of cigarettes whose butt-ends littered the room. Before I could open my mouth, the poet told me to allow him some time, because he had something on his mind. From the way he looked I knew he was spinning a new verse, so I kept quiet. I sat on the chair facing the divan. He finished his cigarette, lit yet another with the butt-end and withdrew into himself as if I wasn't there. Between patting his thigh and picking his nose – and always that cigarette – he went on mumbling to himself. Suddenly he came out of his thoughts to tell me how wonderful a tea would be. Before I could respond he had already resumed his thoughts. Dutifully I went to make the tea. When I came back with it, he barely acknowledged me. I resumed watching him. Suddenly a pack of huge rats, raising a deafening uproar, zoomed diagonally across the room and disappeared in the pile of rubbish heaped next to the cooker. I told the poet what I had seen. He told me that I must be imagining things, because he hadn't seen any rats; surely there couldn't be any here. Yet I noticed that as he lit another cigarette, dug his elbow deeper into his pillow, he pulled the tattered sheet of his divan, protectively I felt, over his feet. Perhaps feeling a bit guilty for keeping me waiting, he said – *Are you doing nicely, my friend?* – but soon he went back to his poetic meditation. I didn't want to disturb him because I knew he was thinking of Brothero-Man. How could you mistake the way he was curving his lips and blowing the air. He wasn't so much mimicking Brothero-Man as he was riding with him in the same galloping motion. Then I heard him as the mumble got louder.

Boy, wasn't he there?
right there, under your very noses
an invisible surveyor marking cities
as if through dense forest and uncharted savannahs
like a white horse with a long flowing mane
galloping through the veins of your city
flickering the icon of his body
& charting

but you look through a microscope
right into the very depths of his pocket
'there there,' you say, 'the map ought to be there.'
how little you know that sizzling of a body
dancing a pure force in twilight
sprinkling ink like rubies along the way
& between walking feet and clicking eyelids
wearing a parchment of a map at one with his body

now you will seize the body
you do that as you please
he laughs, glinting his gold teeth
seeing the floating mirror of his body
stamping space in the speed of his trails.
my lords and ladies, I am afraid
he has bitten off a chunk of your land
& grinning gold with his teeth

I heard a sharp cry from the street below and jumped to the
window. I cleaned the steamed-up panes with my palms and
looked down to see what was happening. The mist was so dense
and the street-lights so dim that they were no more than drops
of yellow in a bowl of milk, but there was no mistaking the van
even though I couldn't see the colour. Just in front of the van

stood three figures in silhouette. Two of them seemed to be barring the way of the third. From their size I could tell that two of the men were the ones in white overalls. But the third? Since they were looking for him, who else could it be but Brothero-Man? The two guys in white overalls seemed to be talking to him, but he suddenly thrust his hands between them and pushed them aside as if cutting through water like a breaststroke swimmer. He began to walk away and then broke into a trot. The two men turned around and ran after him. One of the men in white overalls, the one of towering bulk, lurched forward and grabbed Brothero-Man's jacket collar, while the other man, the thin and tall one, stood in front. Perhaps he was still trying to persuade Brothero-Man to come voluntarily. He, though, jerked himself free from the man who was holding him from behind and head butted the man in front. This I concluded from the way the man in front was holding his head. My brothero certainly knew how to take care of himself. Now he began to trot again, with the man of towering bulk trotting after, grabbing for him, almost flying through the air. Brothero-Man seemed to be trying desperately to stay upright and shake off the man of towering bulk. But the thin, tall man came around and grabbed him by the neck. Brothero appeared to elbow him fiercely and drag the man of towering bulk along the pavement. The tall, thin man was hitting Brothero-Man with a truncheon-like object. He fell to the ground, curling up. Then it was all over and the two guys in white overalls were dragging him towards the van. I shouted to the poet that they were taking away our brothero. He jumped off his divan and we ran out to the street. As we reached the van, a policeman came out of the station, which was just opposite. He focused his torch on the scene and at last we could see clearly what was happening. The two men were indeed the mad-catchers in white overalls. But the third looked like a policeman. It wasn't Brothero-Man. I cursed myself for not realising that it wasn't his style to fight that way. The third man was Jamir Ali. It was a common knowledge on Brick Lane that one day, possessed by the evil bobby-spirit, he had stopped speaking and gone mad. He made himself a police uniform, bought a real-looking helmet and stood outside the station, as if he was a real policeman on duty. He wasn't struggling now, but all the same they dragged him into the van through the backdoor, and slammed it shut. They told the policeman with the torch that there were others still roaming the streets who were madder than the one they'd caught. Then the thin, tall mad-catcher looked at me suspiciously.

*– You can be sure he won't get away. We're here to round up all the loonies. We've our job to do, you know. But specially him – the real Mr Crazy. We'll get him by the time the night's up. We aint buffoons, we have our information. We know he's planning something crazy at dawn. We can't let that happen, can we?* He was about to get into the van but came back to look me up and down closely.

*– What they really call you around here, eh? You don't fool me, mate, we're watching you. But one piece of advice: if I were you I'd stop this walking nonsense. Why did you have to come all this way here to do your bloody walk? It sickens me, it really does.*

They drove away, turning the corner into Fashion Street. The poet went back to his flat and I walked on looking for Brothero-Man. On the way I met Allamuddin Khan – a deadly serious fellow, all-round guru and a nonconformist *par excellence* – buzzing like a queen bee through the haze, surrounded by his young followers. At first he didn't notice me, he was so absorbed in his wise-man role. I caught the name Vatsyayana and thought perhaps he was pep-talking the boys on the delicate art of seduction. Suddenly seeing me so close, he froze with a start. Then, he said abruptly, as if to regain his composure:

*– We must finish our talk on the metrical form of Rabi Thakur's work.* He remained silent for a while, and then smiled

wryly. But he was soon back to his old form again, laying on all
sorts of esoteric wisdom to the bafflement and admiration of his
followers. I thought if the two mad-catchers in white overalls got
to hear him he'd be in real trouble. I told him about them and
Brothero-Man. Allamuddin Khan, despite all his wisdom, looked
shaken.

— *For argument's sake, even if he is mad, what the hell they
think they are up to? We have been living all our lives with so
called mad people, even eating from the same plate. And certainly living in the same house and the same neighbourhood. It
never bothered us. Anyway who can tell who is really mad?*

He wanted to come with me but I told him that I would rather
look for Brothero-Man on my own. Anyway, he told me that he
and his boys would go round looking for him too.

I slipped my hands deep into my pockets, turned my lapel to
cover my neck and walked on. I hadn't gone far when I paused
in front of what had been Naz cinema. Sadly, these days it stood
only as a monument to that bygone celluloid age. At this time of
the night its entrance looked dead except for a few tramps who
lay huddled up in cardboard and rags. But during the day, a
different form of life unfolds in its precincts. Ever since the
cinema had gone bust, there had been a bazaar here. At the
centre of this bazaar was the stall of righteous things. And at the
hub of this stall was the black-beard-and-no-moustache presence of the master of righteous arts himself — Mulana Abdul
Hakim. As I stood there I remembered how Brothero-Man had
rescued me from the trap so cunningly laid by the Mulana. I was
green then in Brick Lane. It was a Friday afternoon and I was
passing the bazaar when I saw the Mulana for the first time.
Seeing him in his righteous pose against the display of Qurans,
calligraphies of divine words, velveted prayer-rugs with images
of Kaba-Sharif, toupees and tabiz, I sensed trouble. I looked
away and quickened my pace, but the very moment I felt his

salaam swoop down on me I knew I was trapped. I had to return
his salaam and approach his stall. Whatever you might think of
him, you had to agree that nobody had a tongue as diamond
sharp as the Mulana. God, how he mows his customers down in
a flash with a regular swipe of it! Then the poor wretches feel
only too happy to buy his righteous merchandise at double its
proper price. No sooner had I reached the stall than the Mulana
unleashed the flourish of his tongue. First, he put me on the hair-
thin bridge that one must cross to reach the gate of heaven.
Underneath the bridge he whipped up the full horrors of hell. I
was balancing most unsteadily on that hair-thin bridge as he
made me feel the heat of everlasting fire and hear the hiss of
swarming serpents down below. The whole game was to do with
righteous debt. If you were found short you'd really had it; no
amount of trapeze skill would see you across the bridge to the
gate of heaven. Sinner that I was, my legs shook. I had the
distinct feeling that I had almost slipped from that bridge,
though I still wasn't prepared to part company with the few
pounds I had for the week if I could help it. In desperation I
looked around for someone or something to rescue me from the
spell of the Mulana. Just to my right was a stall selling Bollywood
posters, but the plumpish heroines in seductive poses and
wearing bathing suits were powerless to rescue me from the hair-
thin bridge. As I dug into my pocket, I knew my pounds were as
good as gone. I could see the impish smile breaking on the
Mulana's lips as he spat out paan-red saliva, waiting to conclude
yet another triumph. But then, as if from thin air, Brothero-Man
came to my side. Mulana Abdul Hakim went pale and silent. Not
daring to look at him and without saying a word, he offered
Brothero-Man a paan from his small tin box. Brothero-Man
snatched the paan off the Mulana most disdainfully and put it in
his mouth. Then he turned his back on the Mulana and grinned,
baring his gold teeth.

*—Brothero, what's this bastard son of Iblish telling you? Can't you see he's a con-man fellow. Most wicked, you see. Always fussing-wussing with his foul talk. Come, brothero, let's run from his ass-like face. Ya ya ya Allah, what a bad-smelling fellow.*

I didn't look back at the Mulana as we walked away together. After that the Mulana didn't bother me any more, but Brothero-Man, despite what he said, always came back to see the Mulana several times a day and chew his paan. Perhaps, with his long black-beard-and-no-moustache, like the Haji, he was good to look at, especially in the setting of his righteous props. But who knows what meaning the Mulana held in Brothero-Man's secret scheme of things. Perhaps, as my friend the poet once told me, in order to stamp his body on the face this foreign city, he needed all these signs.

Hearing me pass, a tramp peered from his cardboard box and asked me if the sun was already up. His friend next to him, the genuine Jack the Ripper, woke up to see what was happening, took a swig from his bottle and once more insisted on his identity. It was well past midnight and I was running out of time to find Brothero-Man before the mad-catchers in white overalls. So I hurried along from the Naz cinema, crossed the road and arrived in front of a pub, which had long since closed. Even on my first day in Brick Lane, this pub struck me as an oddity. It was as I stood looking at it for that first time that Brothero-Man appeared, as he did on so many occasions, by my side.

*—Brothero, just like me, this place is not what it seems. You see, it's an either-neither place. But most interesting. You've to lift the veil-bhorka to see the face. You know what I mean, brothero?* He disappeared quickly again. Well, there's no doubt that behind the veil of a pub it was a different place. Most unlikely and almost hard-to-believe but it was a solid thing. You mustn't laugh when I tell you that the landlord was a puritanical turban-wallah, who served halal beer with samosas to a castaway

clientele who outdid one another in bah-bah over oriental striptease.

Through the rows of cash & carries, the unisex hairdressing salons and then more groceries and restaurants, I finally arrived at the mouth of Brick Lane, its name announced on a black-rimmed white plaque. But where was Brothero-Man? I knew that he wouldn't walk beyond this point because it was the borderline of his territory – and sometimes a territory which had to be defended. In fact, it was once a war zone. Yes, those were the days of cropped-headed-bovver-boots selling *Bulldogs*. They came like a pack of hyenas in broad daylight to raid Brick Lane. They drew blood, oh yes they drew blood, and marched away watched by many panic-stricken eyes. But those were also the days when the workers surfaced from the twilight zones of sweatshops and from the steamed-up kitchens at the backs of restaurants. No matter what the danger, they stood their ground behind the barricade. But always in front, before the assault of the enemy, was Brothero-Man. He stood immobile in the chosen colour of the day with a giant rattan-stick in his hand. Then he was a commandante, my brothero.

Since he wouldn't go beyond this point, there was no need for me go any further. So I turned back. When I looked at the horizon I suddenly became aware that the markings of *our* city were no more than tiny dots in the sea of their strange city. There were the tall glass-faced skyscrapers of the city of London. Even in the mist and darkness they loomed menacingly over Brick Lane. Every time Brothero-Man looked up to see the skyscrapers he became restless. He walked with renewed urgency as if constructing a battlement to safeguard his territory against an advancing enemy.

On my return leg, at the corner of Old Montage Street, I met Asad and his boys in leather jackets. They were patrolling the streets against the raiders of the night. They told me that they

hadn't yet seen Brothero-Man but they had come across the two
guys in white overalls. Some of the boys had wanted to teach the
guys a lesson but Asad had dissuaded them, by reminding them
of the power of the law. The boys moved on and I continued on
my way. As I passed Chicksand Street I saw the mad-catchers
pissing against a wall. I slunk away like a cat. I was once more
following the beaten tracks of Brothero-Man. First, along Brick
Lane, and then the alleyways that merge onto it, but always
checking and rechecking the spots he would have stopped and
looked at. But he was nowhere to be seen, and as a man without
fixed abode, there was no home that I could check. Nor was there
any spot where he slept because he hardly ever slept.

– *So little time, brothero*, he once told me, *so little time for all
the tasks that need completing before they come for you. How
could I waste time in a rubbishy-wubbishy thing like sleeping*.

I went back to the tower block in Hanbury Street, took the
stairs again, and arrived at Munir's and Soraya's flat. It was
nearly two o' clock. When I rang the bell, Munir came bleary-
eyed to open the door. Soraya was just behind, looking anxious.
She asked me if I had found Brothero-Man. I said no, but that
the mad-catchers were still looking, evidently determined to get
him before dawn. Munir asked me if I had eaten anything. I said
I wasn't hungry, but Soraya disappeared into the kitchen and
came back with a plate of rice with an assortment of left-over
curries and dhal and a saucer with two green chillies, pieces of
onion, and some salt. I ate sitting on the sofa. Munir picked up
an old newspaper and turned the pages absent-mindedly.
Soraya looked cold and sad; she cupped her chin, hiding her
mouth and stared down at the floor. Without lifting his face from
the pages, Munir told me how muchTariq was looking forward
to going to the zoo. Both of them insisted that I should spend the
night at their place. But I said no, I had to go my friend the poet's
place. You see, every day like a clockwork, between two and

three in the morning, Brothero-Man never failed to show up at the poet's, bringing him curries and rice. With a grin he would produce biscuits, cakes, bananas and oranges out of his pockets. By this time of night, the poet would be so hungry that he would eat at a furious pace and Brothero-Man would always say – *Sorry, brothero, I'm so late*. Then they would talk and laugh together until dawn when the poet fell asleep on the divan. Brothero-Man would pull the blanket over him and set out to walk yet another day.

When I rang the bell, the poet came rushing because he thought I was Brothero-Man. He was very hungry, pacing the room, puffing his cigarettes.

*– Why doesn't he come yet? I'm so hungry today, my friend. Do you think something might've happened to him? If they take him what will become of me?*

I sat on the corner of the poet's divan, waiting for Brothero-Man. An hour had passed. The poet was getting desperate; he was pacing the room, now and then looking through the window, still oblivious to the quarrelsome rats that had now taken over the room. God, he was so hungry that he even rummaged the pile of rubbish from where the rats had come. But he found nothing that he could eat, so he began licking some sugar from an almost empty packet. When he'd finished this, he burped loudly.

*– You take some rest, my friend. When he comes I'll wake you up.*

I thought of little Tariq – how he must be dreaming of going to see giraffes. I mustn't be late for that. Yes, I could do with some rest.

I lay on the poet's divan and looked up and saw the green and brown patches on the ceiling. The patches of mould were dancing in intricate geometric patterns. I couldn't take my eyes off them because the sudden loops of their curves and the crisscrossing play of their lines were etching the passageways through which so many had come to map the new city. Armies of men, women and children marched shoulder to shoulder like columns of ants. Undaunted, they pushed their way through the mazes, but many lost their way and perished. Some, though, had found their way through the mazes and floated on the deep pools of their toils to arrive at the golden city they had mapped in their dreams. The rats had gone quiet, but the poet was still walking. I could hear the movement of his feet on the loose planks of the floor, making creaking noises. They had a rhythm like the lullabies of wind against the broken latch of the window.

*the poet is calm now after his dinner    he lights a cigarette slumps back into the pillow at the far end of the divan    Brothero-Man pulls the chair very close    almost breathing into the poet's face    they are happy now they are whispering to each other and laughing pressing their hands against their mouths because they don't want to wake me up    they are so considerate my brothero    how nice he looks today in his immaculate white flannel suite and a crimson tie    polished white shoes and his golden teeth    but no broad-brimmed hat today    just as well because a white pagri with a long flowing tail suits him most handsomely    he is so happy now    sweet smile breaking loose on his clean-shaven face    sweet smell of just a touch of musk by and by the time has gone    the poet wants to embrace him to say goodbye but Brothero-Man will have none of it    it's too theatrical    too much fussing-wussing    he breaks into a huge laugh takes out a smooth green apple from his pocket and offers it to the poet saying take care of yourself brothero    wipe that silly sadness off your face    you'll see me again    sure you'll see me again but in a different way    now the poet extends his languorous arm to receive the gift    gently touching the sinuous hand that offers the apple    perhaps despite himself he can't prevent a drop of tears clouding his eyes    but Brothero-Man doesn't have the time for all that    now he needs to walk    how*

*he needs to walk  because the dawn is breaking through the mist
its soft light streaming through the windows with a promise of a
perfect morning    without any ceremony then and just as he has
been doing for years Brothero-Man sniffs the air and lands on
Brick Lane    almost immediately he takes in his stride the
empty thoroughfare  the alleyways  his nimble fingers habitually counting the crystal beads on his tabiz, and one by one he
remembers    Mulana Abdul Hakim's stall    Haji Sahab's
grocery  Zamshed Mia's sari shop  Turbanwallah's pub  the
minaret of the Mosque   children singing rhymes in the play-
ground   odour of spices claiming the alleyways   boys cueing
on the green table  the purring of machines in sweat shops  and
so much more   but the two men in white overalls have already
taken to Brick Lane   they sniff the air sensing Brothero-Man's
presence    they pick up their pace pursuing him through
alleyways like men possessed with a mission of pivotal impor-
tance   they lose him for a while  so they run wildly and emerge
on Brick Lane again through Hanbury Street   whatever the
mad-catchers might think Brothero-Man is not one for running
away  it's simply not his style   within minutes he comes back
to Brick Lane via Old Montage Street  now heading towards the
mad catchers in white overalls   he's already passed the thresh-
old and the supple movements of his feet have reached their
unreachable perfection  whirling and almost floating through
the air  the tail of his pagri fluttering like a sail caught in high
winds  finally they see each other fifty paces apart  the two
men in white overalls pause a second  then rush madly to catch
their mad patient  but Brothero-Man is not running away  only
advancing most delicately towards them in slow motion and
melting in the ether  first his torso  then his hands then his legs
and neck though his white shoes and floating pagri and his
golden grin glide on their own through the air and almost touch
the mad catchers at the corner of Chicksand Street before*

*vanishing completely  leaving the two men standing mute and
frozen*

In the morning I found the poet sprawled next to me on the
divan. He was snoring raucously, an orange filter still squashed
between his smoking fingers. I opened the curtains and let the
soft sunlight drape me with the fragility of muslin, then drew
them back again so the sun wouldn't wake the poet up. I hit the
streets. I don't know why everybody seemed to be staring at me
as I walked through the lane. I went to a corner-shop to buy some
sweets for little Tariq because I knew he would demand them as
soon as he saw me. When I tried to pay, the shopkeeper wouldn't
take any money. He just shook his head in silence, not daring to
look me in the eyes. It was getting late so I didn't waste any time
trying to pay him. Soon I was on my way to Soraya's and Munir's
flat, to pick up little Tariq. He would be all worked up to see the
giraffes. Still, there was time for a quick stop at the Sonar Bangla
for a cup of tea. As I entered, a hushed silence descended on the
cafe. I went to a lonely corner, sat facing the painting of the boat
on the horizon. But the oarsman wasn't singing any more. I was
still puzzled to see that people were staring at me with the same
melancholy eyes as they were in the street. Then Lilu walked in
from the kitchen with a cup of tea in his hand. He set it on the
table in front of me, leaned over and whispered in my ear.

– *Brothero*, he said, *two mad-catchers in white overalls were
looking for you. You got to hide, brothero, you got to hide.*

# THE TOWER OF THE ORIENT

Munir hurried along the corridor as soon as the postman's footsteps faded and Soraya came tiptoeing behind him. He ripped open the brown envelope with nervous fingers. Soraya, sensing the good news, looked up at him so that their eyes would meet in perfect harmony at the moment that revealed that they were to have a flat of their own. Her eyes, grown pallid in the malignity of blue staring eyes, sparkled again and two dimples rippled on her cheeks.

So much time had been spent in dreams, so many dreams had grown stale, waiting for this moment promised all those years ago, the intoxicating moment of taking off from Dhaka airport for this destination of fabled fortunes. Munir once more thought of the dark hole of the sweat shop, among the clatter of machines, and of all those dreamy letters he wrote back home, full of fat creams and princely palaces, grown fancier by the day, while they were living in damp, creeping rot and a riot of rats. It was England. How could he have said they weren't living it up in an opulence beyond all dreams? When his old ma sent letter after letter begging for his return, pleading him for a brief holiday visit so she could look lovingly at his face grown smooth from all that good living, he wrote her lies, a spiral of lies, knowing full well that he couldn't lie to his old ma looking straight in her eyes. Now the promise brought by the envelope meant that he could at last write to his old ma, of a moment of true happiness, without imagining her as an eyeless ghost.

Before Soraya began to think about any of the practicalities of moving, she was already blowing dust off the embroidery frame. The base of the embroidery – a circular piece of stretched calico – sagged at the edges from having lain idle for so long. She stretched the calico and fastened the frame tight with the same tingle in her fingers as when she had first begun. The same outline of a deer in faint pencil sketch stood motionless among flowers in a green forest. The background was already done, only the deer was waiting to come alive. She looped the looping thread, dipped and surfaced, and the colour poured in from the needle. While Soraya lost count of time, humming between the dips of her needle, Munir moved soundlessly as a cat, sensing the surfacing of deep yellow and the wondrous life of the deer from the dancing fingers. But where should it hang in their new flat? Perhaps in the sitting room. You need something really nice to brighten it up. Besides, one must take care to make a good impression on guests. But how can Soraya trust Munir? Honestly, that man is such a show-off. Would he ever miss a chance to swell with pride and blow his wife's trumpet, as loudly as a hawker in a market? Look, it's our Soraya's own work. I bet you've never seen a deer as pretty as this. How embarrassing! It would make Soraya feel like hiding in a sea of grass. No, it should go in our bedroom. Only they, lying side by side, heads slightly raised on the pillows, should look at the yellow deer breathing purple in the dim blue light. Munir would hold the hands which had woven the threads of love and the forest's soft murmur would float into the room with a distant flutter of leaves.

It was a spring day unlike others. The sun poured in, splashing the city with an airy lightness, as if it would take to

wing any minute. They travelled east, deep into the east, through
Sunday's sparsely crowded streets, following the path of the
Thames. There it was – THE TOWER OF THE ORIENT – ash-
coloured, basking in the silvery sun. *Amazing!* said Soraya, still
transfixed by the height of the tower soaring in the sky. *It's so
tall! Back home they simply couldn't imagine our luck. Who
would believe that we're living so high?*

– *Yes*, said Munir with pride. *It's seventeen storeys tall and we
will be right at the top.* He said no more, in fact remained almost
tight-lipped, as though eager to get on with the task in hand. But
the flickers in his eyes were back, and to Soraya they spoke
tenderness in casual looks that lingered a shade longer than the
moments demanded.

From the place where they parked the van, a straight path of
fifty or so meters ran over neatly mown grass to the entrance of
the tower. At least ten times, not always well synchronised, they
shuffled the length of the path, carrying heavy boxes. Munir was
brisk-paced and invariably ahead of Soraya. She plodded
behind, occasionally quickening a gear but never catching up.
On the seventh lap, Soraya suddenly stopped halfway and
looked with amazement at a solitary lilac tree covered in purple
blossom. How can you say that April is the cruellest of months
and the land is the land of the dead? There were lines of daffodils
contemplating in yellow from thin, green stalks. Further away,
she discovered violet, yellow and white patches of crocuses
peering exuberantly up through the uniform green expanse.
Mixing memories and desire – she had discovered that this
strange land had flowers too – made her dreamy-eyed again,
adding to the happiness already bubbling inside. Oh, the
colours, so pretty like a chintz-print wrapped around your body!
She sat down on the soft grassy mound under the lilac tree,
wanting to extend this moment so that a new memory would be
born to drown other memories. She called Munir. *Come, have a*

*look! We are so lucky, aren't we? So many pretty flowers around in this meadow!* Munir came and sniffed the flowers. *They don't smell sweet, do they? What kind of flowers are they? All pretty pretty without sweet smell. I call them heartless flowers.* Soraya was annoyed with Munir for being such a spoilsport, but he saw his own pretty flowers rocking and skipping on her cheek and the chital eyes were as bright as when he first looked at them. He, too, wanted to make a memory of this moment under the lilac tree. Only a blind fool would say that April is the cruellest of months and the land is the land of the dead. Suddenly they heard a loud bang from the paved entrance to the tower. A bottle, perhaps dropped from one of the higher floors, lay shattered in a pool of milk. And they woke up from the dream.

Once all the boxes were piled up near the lift, they counted them. Pleased that they were all there, Munir pressed the button. Within seconds, a metallic cage rumbled in front of them and opened its doors. A fetid smell of urine wafted their way. Munir lifted his chin in stoic indifference and Soraya pressed her nose against the edges of her sari. A glance at the cage told Munir that at least six or seven trips were needed to carry all the boxes up. He decided to go up alone, except for the last trip when Soraya would join him with the remaining boxes. Soraya, all tremulous at the sight of the lift, was relieved that she wasn't to travel in it yet. It looked like a metallic grave, ready to devour her in its airless, timeless trap. She sat on a box and brought out the embroidery from her bag. The legs and the tail and most of the torso of the deer were already frolicking in a sea of yellow as if they couldn't wait any longer for the head to come alive. Not long to go, just few more hours and it would be ready to hang in their bedroom. The dancing fingers were weaving in waves again, dipping and surfacing, and she could hear the lilac calling her from the meadow. She was calm again and ready to take the lift. Then two young boys came by, riding bikes. They stopped just outside the vestibule, staring at her inquisitively. When Soraya glanced at them with a smile, they paddled away as if frightened. How strange, she thought, but then it's only natural that kids should be scared of strangers. Who is not scared of strangers? And these days, Allah, you can't be too careful, all the stories one hears of baby-snatchers and psychopaths and what not. But as soon as she had polished up her English she would make friends with the neighbours, invite them round to teas and dinners. They would be sure to appreciate her samosas, biryanis and sweet breads. After all, she wasn't a stranger, but only coming home.

When Soraya saw that Munir had completed the seventh lap, she followed him in silence into the lift, nose pressed against the sari. Then she thought, what if someone saw her now, what would they think of her? Perhaps the person would smile quietly to himself, thinking, ah the typical underdeveloped type, veil and all, full of savage customs. Or would he realise she was shielding herself from the stench of urine? She decided it would be better not to give a wrong impression on the first day, so she flung the corner of her sari away from her face and held her breath. By the time they reached the fifth floor, Soraya had already given up holding her breath and was gasping. There was so little air and everything was getting dimmer and memories of other times were catching up with her.

Then she was a girl in a red dress among the mango groves, where the rivers flow out to meet the sky. *It's getting dark; already the fireflies are out from the bushes and I haven't gathered the swans in yet. I have to gather them, they're running all over the place and Ma is looking out from the outer fence for them. I must gather the swans, but it is getting so dark. The muezzin is calling for evening prayers, but how could I leave Nilufar, the lazy sod, always falling behind? Believe you me, I could smell the teacher's skinny boy; he was hiding behind the bushes, he was stalking us with his crazy smile. The swans are all over the place, and the muezzin is calling for the evening prayer. I swear that teacher's skinny boy is crazy with his evil eyes. But even aunty Kulsum says it was just a tragic accident, that I, a careless dreamy girl, fell into the well, to the dark dark bottom of the well. There was so little air to breath; the bats were flapping their wings. I swear it was that teacher's crazy boy. He pushed me, giggling crazily. Ma, oh Ma, I can't breath. The muezzin isn't calling any more, he isn't calling any more; the bats are flapping their wings. I must sleep, Ma. Your ma is here, my child, your ma is here. Sleep, girl, sleep, my little piece of the moon, sleep, do you hear the fairies blowing winds? Sleep, girl, sleep.*

Soraya stood stiffly against the tarnished aluminium side of the lift as the droning cables pulled the cage up. But soon she saw the panels changing places and sweat oozed into her lips, adding bitterness to the traces of other memories. She would have vomited right there if it hadn't been for Munir's cold hands pressing on her nape. The lift crawled past a few more floors. Now that Soraya's nerves had eased a little, she looked around and saw the graffiti smeared on the panels in all sorts of colours and calligraphies. There was a profusion of hearts and declarations of love. Some were in clumsy scrolls, others in immaculate strokes: Bob loves Sharon, Julia dreams of Jerry, Arthur kisses Mandy, and Liz hopes to run away with Kevin. Soraya thought of the lilacs, the daffodils and the crocuses, such pretty colours like a chintz-print around your body. No, April can never be the cruellest of months and this land is not the land of the dead. Soraya felt like humming again, her eyes sparkled. They were so lucky, surely they had come to the right place, among so many flowers and lovers' hearts.

On the thirteenth floor, the lift came to a halt and opened its doors. Before them stood an old lady. She looked fragile, bent in an arched stoop, straining her eyes to look up. She had a

serene face shining through the crumpled passage of time; her
eyes looked so tender that they immediately reassured Soraya.
She smiled and almost said good afternoon, but froze at the
sudden glint of horror in the old lady's eyes. She almost
straightened her stooped back, turned brusquely around and
walked away muttering. Soraya couldn't quite make out what
she was saying except for the refrain, hissed through her bare
gums: *God, what's next!* Soraya looked long as the old lady made
her way down the corridor. She felt pity for her, thinking that she
must have gone senile, was perhaps even a bit soft in the head,
but surely she didn't mean any harm. What harm could she
mean? Or perhaps *God, what's next!* was, along with the fetid
smell of urine and the suffocating cage, the dark shadow in the
lovelorn hearts, the thorns on the flowers and the wind of the
cruellest month. She desperately tried to remember the flowers,
but the swoon of the cage had already turned the purple, the
yellow and the white of the meadow into a whirlpool of never-
ending grey. *Oh Allah, so little air, the bats are flapping their
wings, that teacher's skinny boy, giggling so wickedly, the
muezzin isn't calling any more, I must sleep, Ma singing lullaby,
girl must sleep, do you hear the fairy blowing wind? Girl, sleep
girl, but the cruel insistence of God, what's next! Oh Allah, so
little air.* Munir dragged Soraya out of the lift and suddenly she
was back to her senses. She snatched the key from him, ran to
open the door and threw up in the hallway of their new flat.

Munir soaked his handkerchief in cold water and rubbed
Soraya's face and the back of her neck with it; she soon felt better
again. They washed the hallway clean with disinfectant and lit
sticks of incense to drive away any residual smell. Then they set
about unpacking and arranging a few essential things. Munir put
electric bulbs in each room and the corridor, plugged in the
small one-ringed-cooker, which they would use until they got a
proper one with four rings, oven and a grill and all. Soraya

cleaned the bathroom. She hung the towels, arranged combs and kohl on one shelf of the cabinet; on another she put Munir's shaving things. Then she moved to the kitchen, cleaned it spotless, stacked the utensils in the base units, arranged the plates and bowls in the wall cupboard, spoons and knives in the drawers, and the jars of spices on the rack. Once these tasks had been done, she turned the ring on and put the kettle on to boil. She waited intently to hear the bubbles. When she heard them, she smiled. The hiss of the kettle confirmed her sense of being at home, that finally they had a home of their own. She brought the tea into the sitting room and they sat side by side on an unopened box, and the aroma of Darjeeling mixed with the lilacs, the daffodils and the crocuses. Soraya playfully brought up the subject but Munir was already thinking of the decoration and furniture they should have in their new flat. Soraya wanted white walls and red velvet curtains. Munir quite liked the idea of white walls but red velvet was a bit too showy for his taste. Didn't fine cotton give an air of muted elegance? But if Soraya really wanted velvet, he wouldn't object. What he really wanted was a round table. How wonderful it would be to sit around a round table with their friends, Soraya delicately serving the dishes, everybody complimenting her cooking; and in their closeness they would gossip and laugh long into the night.

They continued to clean, unpack and arrange things. Soraya boiled some rice on the one-ringed-cooker and fried canned sardines with spices. She would go shopping tomorrow and cook a proper meal to celebrate their homecoming, but Munir wasn't complaining, in fact, he'd never tasted a better meal. Although made of no more than simple sardines and plain rice, it tasted more delicious than a feast of roasts, kebabs and pillao rice, and he wanted to preserve this flavour for posterity. After the meal Soraya took up her embroidery again. She looped the looping thread, dipped and surfaced, and hummed, swaying her waist-long black hair. *Oh my bosom friend, who plays the reed-flute so near yet so far by the acacia tree*. Munir looked at her, transfixed at the chital eyes sparkling again, as if the malign blues had never touched them, and at the dimples flowing in the waves, dipping and surfacing with the looping thread. Soraya, suddenly conscious of his gaze, stopped and said, *Oh Ma, such deep looks, as if you'd never seen me before*. Without thinking, without even gesturing to each other, they got up together, and holding hands went to the back window and looked at the moonlight playing on the Thames. That moment everything came right between them, and *God, what's next!* disappeared along with memories of other nightmares. Only the lilacs, the crocuses and the daffodils leapt out of the meadow to entwine them with the memories of colour. No. April can never be the cruellest of months and the land is not the land of the dead.

The next day Munir went to work early in the morning. Soraya stayed home, unpacked a few more things, hung the calligraphed name of Allah on the wall, just above the mantelpiece. Then she remembered that she ought to be going shopping.

She stood before the lift and reproached herself for the self-inflicted nausea of yesterday. She convinced herself that the ghost of the past had finally been exorcised, that she was silly to be afraid, that it was time they should have a new beginning. She pressed the button and within a few seconds the lift arrived and opened its doors. She wanted to stride in with confidence, but paused, because there facing her in dripping scarlet, where the lovelorn hearts had been, was the unmistakeable message, inexhaustibly repeated: WOGS OUT PAKIS STINK DARKIS GO HOME. Soraya stood there for a few seconds as if looking beyond the writing to conjure up the memories of flowers. Suddenly she heard the flapping wings of the bats again in the dark dark cavern and *God, what's next!* mowing down the flowers with savage sickle swipes. She turned and ran inside her

flat again. She sat on the bed, her whole body shaking as if in the
throes of malaria, and her head was buzzing with so many
questions, but who would listen to her questions? And answers,
if there were any answers, what sense would they make?

She got up and went to the back window. On the other side of
the river, in the distance, she saw the grand whiteness of
Greenwich staring at her mockingly. From this side of the river,
there were tall skyscrapers with gleaming glass, grotesquely
shooting up in the sky. On the Thames, heavily-laden barges
and tourist cruise boats were going to and fro on the calm waters.
Absent-mindedly, she moved from the window, took up her
embroidery frame again and did the looping loop, dipped and
surfaced. How nicely the deer's head was coming along, and the
flowers were still swaying their heads in the meadow. Yes, they
hadn't mown them down yet. Soraya regained her calmness. She
wasn't going to give in so easily. A few graffiti weren't going to
stop her, though she could wait to take the lift in her own good
time. Meanwhile, it was simply a matter of using the stairs, tiring
though they were, but she was in no hurry. She took the stairs,
sliding her left hand over the metallic handrail, gently but
rhythmically making her way down. In the obstinate silence,
each bend of the stairway, each new floor murmured sinister
possibilities. There was relief when nothing but emptiness and
silence greeted her, until she left the fourteenth floor and turned
the bend for the thirteenth. On the landing, a bulldog sat facing
the stairs, as if it had been expecting her for some time. Its eyes
had an unmistakable tenderness, peering out of its wrinkled
face. No doubt a much loved pet. She would pass by it slowly or,
if necessary, she would even pat the gentle brute. But a savage
glint flashed in its eyes, so familiar that it could well have been
a playback of yesterday on the thirteenth floor. Then the bulldog
began to growl. Soraya felt a chill gust gnawing down her spine.
Oh no, the bats were flapping their wings again. She heard the

whispers echoing from the silence of the night and the bulldog rasping *God, what's next!* and mowing down the flowers with sickle swipes. *God, what's next!*

Soraya's hand lost its grip on the handrail. She turned and ran up the stairs; the bulldog followed her growling and whispering. Now there were so many voices, all giggling, mocking the silence, and leaping out to spread their nets all around her path. She somehow opened the door and slumped on her bed. She realised how cunning this trap was, how truly she was caught in its web.

She rolled on the bed, walked the length of the flat, counting time. If only Munir was here; together, surely together, they would be able to face up to the situation. It would be nine before Munir was back. Soraya scoured the boxes containing the leftover food they had brought with them. Besides sardines and rice, she found a few eggs, potatoes and a handful of lentils. She must cook a nice meal for him. She put all her imagination and skills to conjuring up a perfectly tuned korma dish with the eggs and potatoes, fried the lentils in butter to make a savoury dhal, and prepared pillao rice to go with them. Still an hour to go before nine. She took up the embroidery, which was nearly complete, except for the eyes. But the deer without eyes nervously fluttered its horns, desperate to get away, perhaps sensing a dangerous carnivore. But what could it do without eyes? Soraya flung the frame face down on the floor. She couldn't bear to look at it, not at the deer without eyes, not any more. She went to the rear window and looked at the Thames. Its banks, edging the murky waters, brooded in gloom. She tried to imagine the flowers, but other memories were already dancing on the graves of the lilacs which were swallowed up by the dead land from which they had sprouted. Is April really the cruellest of months? Soraya looked at herself in the mirror. I mustn't let Munir see me like this, I will make him happy, always together, we will be happy. She rubbed coconut oil into her waist-long black hair, plaited it, and girlishly tied it in a blue chiffon scarf. How nicely it goes with the blue sari. Munir will be pleased, so pleased; he will stare at me lost in a dream. Soraya brought her eyes closer to the mirror. Yes, they mustn't carry the burden of terror. She adorned them with long strokes of coal-black stibium, dabbed a crimson circle on her forehead. Should she even redden her lips with lipstick? No, that would be going too far.

It won't be long now, only fifteen minutes to go until the dead sound of the final stroke of nine. It'd be better to go out and wait by the lift, so she stands by it with the immobility of a gecko, alerting her ears so that nothing should escape her, not even a tiny sound from the ground floor. She mustn't miss the trip Munir is destined to take. Despite her desire to speed things up, the seconds and the minutes are dying a prolonged death all over Soraya. She paces the corridor, moves from one side of the lift to the other. She is weighed down by the silence, as if everybody is holding their breath for the inevitable, the event that will take place on the thirteenth floor. Soraya can hear the flapping of the bats and see the scarlet drips; it will happen at the dead sound of the final stroke of nine. She is now pacing erratically and humming a breathless hum. She would scream for help, but who is there to help her, since everybody is holding their breath for the inevitable to happen? Oh Allah, it's so hot, it's burning. Sweat pours through her stibiumed eyelashes in kohl-black streams to her lips. I must go down, even if the chamber of death swallows me up, I must warn Munir what awaits him at the thirteenth floor. Then at the dead sound of the final stroke of nine the silence is finally ruptured and Soraya hears the pull of the cable. The cage is moving, yes, it's moving with a swishing hum, ascending at an unfaltering pace; it is getting louder and more distinct by the second; it must have passed the halfway mark by now; in only a few more seconds Munir will pass the thirteenth floor and will be safely home. Then suddenly the lift stops – is it the thirteenth or the twelfth or the fourteenth floor? It doesn't make any difference because it stands there lost in the hush of the night, as if everybody has retired after their expectant vigil, after the inevitable has happened. Soraya pushes the button, the cable starts to pull once more, the cage is humming the whisper and the growl, *God, what's next!* and the scarlet drips are dripping on the dead land, where they have mown down the flowers with savage swipes of sickles.

# THE FABLED BEAUTY OF THE JATRA

A tall thin man slopes down the bank in the mist, lunges the sampan into the lagoon and clambers onto the stern-post. Here the water is too shallow for the oars. So two men, one on each side of the rear deck, use long bamboo poles to punt the sampan out of the lagoon into the deep dark water of the river. Then they take to their oars as the sail, rolled up around its beam, stays dangling halfway up its long soaring mast. Each movement of the oars, tussling against the dead-weight of the water, drains the meagre strength of the oarsmen. They pant and pray for the wind. But only now and then a ripple languorously ruffles the water. The sampan gently rolls sideways and moves slowly upstream through the haze hovering low over the river.

— *O my Beauty, it saddens my heart to see you so pale.*

Nataraj leans forward to offer the chillum replete with black essence of hemp to Badal. He takes it between his palms and bows to the old tiger.

— *So kind of you, dear Tiger; it's just my nerves, I'll be fine once we set sail.*

Badal closes his eyes, takes a long drag and passes the chillum on to Manik, who plays the young princess – his rival – in tonight's jatra. The troupe is well settled in the inner sanctum of the sampan, circulating the chillum, whiling away the time, on the way to the venue, which is a long way off, in the depth of the great marshland. The dashing young prince, handsome with long curly hair, walks around the circle of smokers in his bejewelled sandals. Then he sits cross-legged between the stricken beauty and the voluptuous princess. He leans over to the beauty, lovingly lifts his delicate hands, dabbing at the gathering sweat with his soft white muslin scarf.

— *What's the matter with you Beauty? I've never seen you like this before. What's bothering you?*

Badal doesn't look up at the tender gaze of the prince. He casts his mournful eyes on the dark patches under the hanging taper in the middle of the circle.

— *You know, Prince dear, how I hate all these beginnings and settings off. I'll be fine once we set sail.*

The matted sadhu, reclining on a round pillow next to the tiger, takes a prolonged drag, smoke shrouding the taper light. Then he booms into laughter as the chillum passes hands.

— *I see dark foreboding, my Beauty. Be careful, it's far too dangerous a game.*

Badal, without the slightest change of his posture, retrieves his hands from the prince's tender caress and receives the chillum from the tiger. He looks at the burning ember of the black hemp before reclining back on his pillow and invites the smoky aroma to furrow into the hub of his senses. He is beginning to feel good despite the damn echoes, the contour of that other face that will be his for ever. Yes, you can't fool him, can't hide from the venerable sadhu. Oh how he has a way of digging his eyes into the very depths of your soul. Badal looks up; a glance passes between himself and the sadhu, mutely capturing the anxiety of that perilous transformation.

— *O wise Sadhu, why do you say these things? You know very well I'm too insignificant an actor to command a role. I'm simply played like a puppet on a string.*

— *Yes, I know, my Beauty, yet all actors dream of playing God, to give life to a puppet. Don't they?*

Outside the oarsmen are plunging their broad-bladed sculls into the dead water. Now that the mist has thinned out, the familiar bends of the river are coming into view faster than the flicker of their eyelids. Yet, they are not moving the sampan any faster. Just as before, they simply cut a sluggish course, though now they move along the trail of the sun, glowing red on the water. The prince opens the shutter of the awning and looks out over the vast expanse of the river. As far as he can see, there is nothing but solitude hanging on the placid water, except for a huddle of dinghies in the distance. They seem to be gathered around an invisible net – perhaps cast to catch the creatures of the deep. Suddenly the tiger jerks his head up from his slumber and roars. He hasn't had his morning feed yet; he is terribly hungry.

Everybody knows that it is far too dangerous to keep the tiger hungry so late in the morning. But what can be done about it? Today, even the kitchen boy has taken to the oars, because there is no wind, and still the men can do no more than wrench the sampan ahead by bitter inches. Taz, the princess, always so eager to oblige, sets off without any prompting. She fetches in a clay bowl the syrupy breads, which are sculptured into birds and beasts and leaves and flowers. In between the chillum, they dolefully grind the crusts of the breads and strain their ears to listen to the ripples breaking on the frame of the sampan.

Nobody is taken by surprise when the sadhu suddenly begins chanting, whirling his matted locks, and the tiger jumps onto the raised platform, violently tilting the sampan. He totters unsteadily, growls, wags his tail, and jumps down ferociously from the platform to perfect his lethal pounce. The sadhu raises himself to his feet and circles the mad tiger, chanting and thumping his feet. The tiger is mesmerised and submits like a cat, purring into a ball. The princess lifts her head from the pillow to glance coquettishly at the prince, fluttering her eyelids. She coos a nimble melody, dances around the mast, jingling her ankle bells. The prince, enchanted, shakes his head to the rhythm. He pretends to surprise the princess from behind the mast; they giggle shamelessly and, holding hands, go out for an illicit rendezvous on the foredeck. The mist has now totally disappeared and the sun blazes on the shimmering water. From behind the hanging trees, the villages, with clusters of mud-huts and golden hayricks, are clearly visible now. The beauty, saddened by the departure of the prince and Taz, falls into a melancholic mood. She imagines their amorous play under the infernal sky and slowly drifts into a sleep. The sadhu stops chanting and whirling, squats beside the beauty, looking at her with rare tenderness. The tiger, too, uncoils himself to sit beside the beauty. He and the sadhu look at each other in silence, and together at the beauty.

How not to remember the season when the company first played their most popular jatra – *The Beauty*! It was then that Badal – a slender-framed boy with exquisite gestures – fell under the spell of jatra. During their week-long season in the marshland that year, they remember how Badal followed them from venue to venue – sometimes even risking his life on a dangerous crossing on a banana-raft – and how he always kept his unblinking eyes glued on the stage. They cannot bear to look at the beauty any more – who is breathing softly on the pillow – so they turn their heads, because, despite being adepts at the simulation of many complex emotions on stage, they cannot hold back their tears.

How long? Yes, it has been more than ten years that they have been travelling together, forming a tightly-knit company, where Badal plays heroines and Manik – the other boy – takes on the other female roles, with Nataraj in support and the sadhu – who is always cast in the role of a sadhu. The tiger purrs like a cat and the sadhu shakes his matted locks. But soon they become quiet again, because they do not want to wake the beauty up. So they only look at each other and communicate mutely their anxiety over Badal and his strange moods. But what can they do? Perhaps, if they tell him that giving up the female roles is not the end of everything, and show him the possibility of other roles – for example, the depths to be found in some male characters – they may be able to convince him that he can always remain a part of the company.

The wind sweeps in, stirring the water; the sampan bobs and rolls on the waves and the sampan-men rush to hoist the sail. Pushed along by the wind swirling against the sail, the sampan is set on a steady course, now only guided by a solitary man at the helm. Everybody, except the beauty, leaves the sanctum under the awning and rushes to the foredeck. The tiger roars fiercely, sending shivers down the waterways into distant villages. The sadhu flings himself into the river with a ball of old butter tucked into his throat. He floats on the water, hanging by the helm, while exercising his vocal reach with a ballad for the forlorn beauty. Princess Taz rolls her eyes, flutters her eyelids and curves her lips to achieve that all too familiar coyness – so obvious even to a slumbering audience, yet not vulgar. Then she taps her flowered feet, ringing her anklets; she is in love, dancing around the awning. The prince, oblivious to his bride – the beauty – rises to the provocation with manly gestures. He seems hopelessly seduced. He stalks the princess with his dreamy eyes, catches her like a wild prey and lowers his lips. They almost touch, her pouting lips quivering with excitement, waiting for his virile caresses. But at the last minute the prince freezes as if a sudden gust of wind has brought him that unmistakable perfume, reminding him of the beauty. He looks away from the princess, and walks desolately back under the awning. The mournful ballad of the sadhu has quietened the ferocious tiger; he is now licking his paws under the triangular shade flung from the sail. The princess thumps her ankles, producing an angry, discordant jingle with her bells. The tiger, disturbed, his whiskers stiffening to the sky, leaps up to sniff the air. And the sadhu breaks off half way through his long modulation.

It is the end of the third act. The forlorn beauty strolls among the wild mango blossom. Her mynah bird, which had flown away years ago, comes back to sit on her shoulder again. The bird sings of the vast kingdoms, exotic palaces and fabulous princesses it has seen on its long flights across seven seas, but nowhere has it seen a beauty who surpasses its beloved beauty. The beauty picks a passion flower, tucks it between the silky coils of her bun and slowly emerges from her melancholia. She then ambles to the secluded pond by the chestnut tree, smears sandalwood paste on her soft skin and bathes herself, washing her long black hair with the lather of soap-nut. Her bright almond eyes, which are exquisitely upturned, glitter again under the arched brows, now accentuated with black powder. She is herself again, the beauty born to enchant a handsome prince.

Without anybody noticing, the sun has already tilted towards the western sky. From the sandy shores along the banks, a flock of wild geese flap their wings and take off into the clear blue sky. The kitchen boy leans against the awning and decants a stream of dreamy notes from his flute into the gentle breeze. The sampan veers off the main river into a narrow channel and enters the great marshland. The men take down the sail in this densely clotted waterway saturated with tangled vegetation. They take to their punts again; only the rare clear patches afford the luxury of the oars.

It is a pleasant and a mellowing afternoon. The troupe move to the foredeck. They repose on an arabesqued carpet: the prince and the princess recline on the plumed pillows; Nataraj sits cross-legged and the sadhu adopts his accustomed lotus posture. They sip spicy tea and savour the coconut breads. Nataraj – the hempmaster – replenishes the chillum with fresh hemp and charcoal. He lights the chillum, using a lump of burning incense, and passes it around anticlockwise with the inclined gesture of deference. Then the sadhu prompts them into a game of dice. They implore Badal to join them. They tell him how the game can't be played without him, because they are stuck for a pair of hands. They are thinking, with pain in their hearts, of what they can do to take his mind off his brooding and frightening silence. Badal stares blankly at the throbbing green of the swamp, speckled with lilies, as if he hasn't heard the chorus of voices behind him. He runs his tongue over his dry lips, moistening them, before turning to face them with an apologetic smile. He nods with gratitude for the loving care shown by his dear friends and hurries under the awning.

He enters his cubicle, hangs the mirror from the spine of the awning and sets out to do his make-up. Isn't it far too early for that? Yes, he knows that well – it will take a few more hours of punting to reach their destination, to the stage crowded with adoring male eyes. Yet he must begin as early as this, because he doesn't want to take any chances, for everything must be right for the last performance. The hemp and the incense and the perfume of sandalwood sets him in the right mood. He takes a deep breath, inhaling the feminine aura, and proceeds with his visible transformation in front of the mirror.

She looks and looks in the mirror until she sees the bubble of her own face floating away into that other face – perfectly oval in cream-rose, around two large, dark, almond eyes – which the fans adore and are hopelessly in love with. She feels dreamy, imagining the passion in their eyes caressing her body as she extends her delicate, lac-lacked, painted feet to descend from the sampan. The beauty puts away her mirror, rests her head on the round pillow and carelessly abandons herself to the man, who, always from the first row, stealthily savours even the most awkward of her feminine gestures with the  timid brown of his eyes. Oh how it tingles her sensual antennae to delirium! As she combs her long black hair, how the beauty loves to dream that handsome face, ablaze under long curly hair, awaiting her with a garland of jasmine as soon as the sampan moors at the ghat. But why is he so shy? Why does he remain almost invisible? Yet his manly odour shadows her from venue to venue across the marshland. Every time she is on stage, and in between snatches of stylised dialogue and songs in treble, she casts her fleeting glances at the handsome-man-with-long-curly-hair, and he averts his eyes or drops his eyelids. Oh how strange, how unbecoming of him to be so shy, yet he can't fool her, she knows it's only a pretence, for she can feel the throbbing of his passion oozing through his closed eyelids and breathlessly derobing her of her silk blouse and the innumerable pleats of her sari. Who else could it be but him who sends her scarlet saris with tight-fitting blouses, foreign lipsticks, and delicate underthings? The beauty takes the perfumed paper from the secret chamber of her bosom and inhales to delirium the indelible traces of that strong, virile hand which has written: *Beauty, oh my dear Beauty, you move as gracefully as an elephant*. Nobody else but the hand-some-man-with-long-curly-hair could have written that. But why is he so mysterious, so cruel, tormenting her with his games of shadows? The beauty dabs the globules of sweat gathered on her face and reapplies layers of talcum and rouge. Perhaps this time, no, she is sure, call it feminine intuition or what you will, yes, he is going to reveal himself to her in a grand theatrical gesture and propose their eternal elopement. She is not one for drab ceremonies and sombre exchanges of brides. No. It will be a carnival of merriment with profusion of laughter amidst dancing, singing and fireworks.

The mournful dusk has set in on the marshland. The troupe has gathered in the inner sanctum; the sampan enters the forest of tall marsh reeds with swaying white flowers. The punters are hurrying up to the stem-post, digging in their punts and pushing towards the stern-post. The sampan is wriggling ahead through the haunting rustles of the reeds.

They have all gathered around the edge of the shadow cast by the taper lamp. Nataraj – the hempmaster – ever mindful of his duty, ceremonially replenishes the chillum with potent black essence and begins the last round before arriving at the ghat. When the sadhu offers the chillum to the figure to his left, a pair of mysterious hands emerges from the shadow. The hands receive the chillum with the customary deference and disappear in the shadow again with a jingle of glass bracelets. Even though they are hallucinating slightly under the narcotic spell of the chillum they do not fail to notice the shapely plumpness of the hands, their silky smoothness so exquisitely feminine.

– *Is it a new make-up or what?* Nataraj asks. There is no response from the shadow, only an echo of silence can be heard. Then a deep breath drags the chillum and releases a dense cloud of smoke into the tiny pool of the taper light. *It is not a make up, Nataraj. What we behold is the most natural and tender attribute of a lady in her prime*, says the sadhu. *Is it you, Badal?* Nataraj asks again the figure in the shadow. Still there is no response. The sadhu gently taps Nataraj on the shoulder. He understands the message and slumps back on his pillow in a deep meditative mood.

Soon all the actors retire to their cubicles to spend some solitary moments on their own. Although it is a ritual, it gives the actors their last chance to go over their roles, to drill their minds into the souls of the characters, and prepare for their metamorphosis on the stage. But for the beauty everything is in a strange muddle today. Doesn't she pride herself with the art of putting on a sweet smile even when burdened by a bitter anguish in her soul? But how she is fumbling today at the simple task, rehearsed so many times, of transforming the woman in herself into an actress, because the fine line between them has blown away like husks of rice in the wind. Despite everything, the beauty doesn't doubt the passion that still hums in her soul. How can she deny the feelings that make her tremble for his virile caresses, for the tang of his salty odour and the breathless whispers in her ears between endless nights of passion? Oh that handsome-man-with-long-curly-hair. Should she reveal her man to her comrades? She knows they are not going to laugh at her; they care far too much for that. The prince is sure to hold her hands and the others will look at her lovingly and nod their heads as though they are unreservedly there for her. But who can prevent them thinking that she is falling to pieces: inventing some fancy man in her moonstruck imagination? Surely, she doesn't want their pity. But how can she convince them that he is real, as real as the pink butterfly resting, as it always does, at the end of her long index finger. The beauty strains her eyes to see the face once more in the mirror, as the taper is getting dimmer and drowning in its own waxy grave. Outside, despite their melody, the elements have assumed once more their darker secrets, and the reeds are now lashing mercilessly against the sampan and whispering the fearful lament of the marshland. She is trembling and lapses into a swoon. Whatever others might think, it doesn't make any difference, because she is convinced that he is there waiting, as ever, and without any reserve for her. But if she is only a hocus-pocus and make-believe beauty, would she deserve his love? She desperately presses her palms against her ears to throttle the insistent whispers, the cruel taunts of the reeds. No no no it doesn't matter a bit, not to him, not to her handsome-man-with-long-curly-hair. Surely he can see through all these simulations the heart of a woman in love. Yes, my darling, it's you who is always on the first row, how you touch my soul even if you don't reveal yourself to me. I don't mind that, for I can sense your love pouring into me through the unspoken channel between us. Please, please, don't

leave me all alone, what else can I be but the beauty. Yes, I knew
you wouldn't leave me, my darling.

The sampan has emerged from the forest of reeds; it is now
making its way through a garden of lotuses. The sadhu has raised
his sombre voice; it is vibrating the sampan and the moonlight
is caressing the tangled green of the lotuses. It is the prelude to
the final act. No doubt, at this point the audience will have been
rapt in attention, with their hearts heavy with sadness – and
perhaps almost verging on tears. They know that the prince is
still infatuated by the princess, but the beauty hasn't given up
on her love for the prince; she is determined to prove it to him
in some ultimate gesture.

Through the zigzag path in the forest the prince has gone for
a secret rendezvous with the princess. The beauty, despite her
sadness, is keeping a vigil. It is getting dark and the silent odour
of tigers hangs perilously under the dense canopy. The dusk is
well past. Why hasn't the prince returned yet, the beauty
wonders. She is getting worried. There are tremulous cries of
deer and the monkeys are howling. She can sense the prowling
of tigers nearby. She is desperate, but what can she do? She is
running, her long black hair flowing in the wind; she is calling
out to him with all her strength. But he can't hear her. Almost as
a last resort, she releases her mynah bird to sing the message.
The mynah bird soars above the canopy, swoops down into the
forest, looking for the prince.

Finally on a narrow path, between dark thickets and through
tiny gaps in the canopy, the prince hears the mynah singing and
calling for him. Suddenly being aware of the danger, he sets off
in panic, the branches of the shrubs whiplashing him from all
sides, but he soon emerges out of the dark forest into the
clearing. But there is no escape route, except through the lake
in front, and the prince jumps into it without thinking of the
consequences. As expected, the tiger too leaps out of the forest

behind the prince and composes himself at the edge of the lake as if he has all the time in the world. Before he can weigh the situation with a certain measure of calmness, the prince finds himself trapped among tendrils of lotuses; he now resigns himself for the claws of the tiger to pounce on him at any minute. But the beauty rushes, with her sari dishevelled and flowing in the wind, through the moonlight, and stands between the tiger and the prince. She begins to sing, as sweetly and as melancholy as she can muster, imploring the tiger, calling him dear brother, asking him not to harm her beloved. She promises the tiger that she will do anything for him in turn, anything he cares to name. The tiger seems to be mesmerised, purring gently, listening to the beauty intently, as if heeding her call. Like all good princes before him, who have been carried away on impulse, the prince now sees through his foolish infatuation and begins to regret his betrayal of the beauty, of her pure, selfless love.

At this point the audience will have somewhat eased their painful entanglement with the high melodrama, because they have sensed a happy conclusion, a final reconciliation between the estranged lovers. Suddenly, his instinct getting the better of him, the tiger growls, sending the wary deer galloping through the dark thickets and the monkeys screaming in cacophony amongst the tall canopy of the forest. He is about to pounce. Obviously, the tiger doesn't want to harm the beauty but she doesn't move. It is far too late for him to resist the savage call of the wild. He assumes the ferocity befitting the king of beasts, extends his massive paws and leaps in a giant arc, aiming at the prince. But the beauty, true to her love to the last moment, shields him with her own body.

After the brief commotion which the kill of the tiger invariably causes, the forest regains its silence again, except for the rustles of dry leaves as a deer forages through the undergrowth, and the creaking of a branch as a monkey leaps to reach a succulent leaf. There is nothing that the prince can do except gather the beauty from the streams of warm blood saturating the roots of floating vegetation, as the tiger disappears into the forest with tears in his eyes. Now the prince is tightly holding the mangled body of the beauty against his own, becoming red with her blood and wailing madly. The mynah bird hovers above, singing mournfully for the beauty, promising her that it would never fly away from its captivity to her heart. As ever, the audience will not have failed to join them in a profusion of tears. It is, after all, a tragic jatra.

The rehearsal is over and the troupe is almost ready for their first night in the marshland. The sampan has entered a clearing and the men have taken to their oars; the moonlight is still playing with the ripples of water. All the actors, except Badal, have gathered on the foredeck.

Nataraj is shaking his head and muttering to himself. Manik is gazing blankly at the stars floating on the water. The prince is pacing restlessly the length of the foredeck. And the sadhu slowly breaks into a sombre requiem for their beloved beauty. He whirls his locks, goes around the sampan in his saffron, burning incense. Then he offers a handful of rice to the water for the safe passage of the soul of their departed comrade while saying: *Dear Badal, may you dance in heaven for the delights of the gods so that they may grant you the secret desires of your heart*.

Once he has completed his priestly tasks, the sadhu hangs the incense pot from the mast-yard and slowly moves over to Nataraj. He squats beside Nataraj, touches his fingers to commune with him, and looks at him with watery eyes as if to say: oh dear old tiger, my heart breaks for you, what cruel fate has decreed that you should play a real tiger, because the beauty wanted to be a real beauty, just as she was in the jatra, and stage her last act in the opaque depths of the water. *Don't cry, my old*

*friend, yours is a supreme sacrifice – you became a savage beast
so the beauty wouldn't wither away at the end of the jatra.*

Suddenly, the prince stops his pacing and looks over the
awning at the infinite expanse of the marshland, which is now
swallowing the gleam of moonlight in its dark, tangled vegetation. He closes his eyes, opens them again, shakes his shoulders, just to make sure that he is not dreaming, because he is
seeing the silhouetted figure of the beauty, serenely reposed on
a raft, emerging from the forest of reeds, and the handsome-
man-with-the-long-curly-hair is punting her away over the
dancing lotuses.

The sampan is almost within the sight of its destination. All
the actors, except of course Badal, remain on the foredeck. The
sadhu is still wrapped around with ceremonial saffron. Nataraj,
the prince and Manik are dressed in freshly pressed white. The
sadhu flings back his locks and stoops his shoulders, holds his
breath, closing his eyes. The rest, without a word between them,
put their arms around one another in an embrace, feeling bound
together by the sandalwood memories of the leading lady. Then
they begin to move: thumping feet, clapping hands, shaking
their heads and chanting the closing chorus. In a matter of
seconds they gather momentum and go round and round in
circles, still thumping and shaking and chanting, into an ecstasy
at the fabled fame of the beauty who was the most beautiful of
all. The sampan-men keep their nerves at the fearsome spectacle
and the sampan slithers on at the cutting of the oars. Not far in
the distance, cymbals and kettledrums can be heard among the
hum of restless fans. They are already well settled on their
cushions of sweet, fuming hay, staring at the empty stage, and
wondering why the sampan is late today in bringing the actors
for the jatra.

# MEETING AT THE CROSSROADS
*for Alicia*

Sliding in half slumber between bittersweet memories of Isabel and news of war in so many places, he catches the weather forecast, announcing the imminent fall of snow. He tries to open his eyes, but they close like the automatic shutter of a camera, and once more he finds himself in the dance of darkness. When he wakes again, he tucks his feather-quilt into a tightfitting capsule, but the ferocious cold bares its fangs against the panes, and the radio has gone dead at the hour preset on the automatic timer. Finally, now that the snow is about to fall, he feels that the moment has arrived for him where, without a sense of regret or nostalgia, he can tell himself that he has left behind that other place where monsoon rains sing on pomegranites in the night. Yet, he is not in a mood to welcome it. No matter how hard he tries, he cannot bear to think of leaving his first footprints on the snow without Isabel beside him.

When Isabel left early that morning, he'd wanted to come to the station, but she insisted on taking her leave from the hall of residence. Yet, how can he not recall her slender figure shivering under the carapace of a long coat, cigarette burning between her tense fingers, its smoke mingling with the floating mist of the hour?

– *Only a few days in London*, she'd said. *Some urgent appointments to attend to.*

– *At least you could leave a phone number*, he'd pressed.

– *Dulal, trust me*, she said, *I'll phone you back, I can't really...*

*I'll explain when I get back. Must go now*, and then simply a casual goodbye.

He turns in his bed, plays with the radio tuner. The temperature is sliding down, the forecaster is getting delirious, her perky tone is conjuring up luminous drifts of snow on endless meadows. But why hasn't she rung? He'd waited by the phone for hours; even at midnight he'd gone down in the lift, chain-smoking as he circled the cubicle for god knows how many times, but she never phoned. Something must have happened to her; it is not like Isabel not to phone, she knows how he suffers from anxiety, and why all that secrecy? Not even a slight hint to him. He would have understood, whatever the reason, but the casualness with which she said that final *chao*, as if she didn't care at all. She could have trusted him a bit. *Together, surely, together, dear Isabel, we could sort these things out*.

She had looked anxious even before the term ended. Scattered piles of papers and opened books, with neat underlined passages, lay on her desk untouched for days. She seemed to have lost interest in her work, had hardly gone out, only sat in the dim light by the window, looking without looking at the clouds gathering and breaking into fragments. Sometimes she had looked the whole day into the dull light of winter, at the line of leafless trees that divided the University from the barren farmlands. She hadn't laughed even when she'd seen a student mimic the *singing-in-the-rain* act and fall headlong into a puddle. He'd wondered then what was the matter with her, because he hadn't seen her that way before. At first he was worried for her, but soon a more personal sense of anguish overtook him. Why was she keeping him in the dark?

One night he'd come back late to their small study-bedroom on the fifteenth floor. He'd expected Isabel to be asleep, but he found her seated in the dark, except for a shaft of light which had sneaked through the folds of the curtain, lighting up a wisp of her brown hair. He was seized by the need to see her face, made so memorable by the way she moved her long brown hair as she looked up with her sepia irises, but her cold immobility only reminded him of the smell of corpses rotting in the paddy fields. Pushing aside that grim memory, and now more concerned for Isabel than his own feelings, he had gone behind her and combed his fingers though the thick texture of her hair. She'd rested her head on the back of the chair as if the warmth of his touch shooed away some demon. *You're sweating, what's the matter with you, Isabel?* he'd asked. She lifted her head, took his fingers into hers, caressing. *Come and sit by me, hold me tight,* she'd whispered. *Hold me tight, Dulal. Nothing's wrong. I was only thinking it can't go on like this, it's too bad, I've got to do something.*

That night he'd learnt of her trip to London, a mere sixty miles from Colchester, but she seemed to have gone to a different world, somewhere beyond him. Perhaps she was haunted by her memories – the lot of exiles – where one was forever on a sand dune so long that the horizon appears further in the distance than the flight of a condor. Yes, the coming together of the Andes and the Himalayas. He tries to remember who pulled their legs on the night they had danced so close to each other that the odour of their bodies drew them together like bees to pollen. Between the dances, the clink of cool glasses of beer had blown away the distance between what were almost the furthest points on earth. *Salud compañero*, Isabel said. *It's true; only in a metropolis like this can we meet from the far-flung corners of the earth.*

After the rage and anguish of that more recent night, Isabel had suddenly looked so tired, lapsing into silence. He wanted to ask her many questions. *Tell me the full story, Isabel. What's really bothering you. Why are you going to London? Please don't leave me out. Together we can always overcome these things.* But seeing her in that state he couldn't bring himself to push further, burden her with his own anxieties. He put a pillow gently under her head and covered her with a blanket. How untroubled Isabel looked in her sleep. This is the way he wants to frame her, in the simplicity of black and white, and always at that moment when she was so close to him that they rose from their bodies and went the other way together. It was dusk, he remembers; they were walking through the woods overlooking the campus. Isabel was whispering in his ear in her own self-absorbed way, yet her warm breath alerted him to their desperate need for one another, holding hands, fingers entwined. Isabel told stories and he listened. There, for the first time, he learnt that she too was a fragment, scattered from a tragedy born of wild hopes to drift through the opaque lights of the metropolis.

*Yes, in a way we expected it*, she told him, *yet we couldn't quite grasp the enormity of it when it came. Perhaps I was too stunned, the only thing I could do was curl up in my bed and fall asleep; only the damn phone screaming the house down woke me up. It was Mama at the other end. I'll never forget the panic in her voice. 'It has happened and everything is over,' Mama told me, 'Isabel please, it's not the time to argue; leave the house by the back door, take the small road facing the cordillera; I've arranged with your uncle Raul; he will take you across to the other side'.* But Isabel couldn't move, she'd sat there on the rocking chair that Abuela so lovingly left her, thinking of the tall eucalyptus and the blossoms of that spring... Mama and Papa were closing their eyes after the picnic; she was frolicking among the bushes with a butterfly net. Suddenly she saw a yellow butterfly flap off from the thorn of a cactus. No sooner had it taken to the air, she followed it into the forest, not noticing the dull shade of the canopy or the drab moss on the ground, for all she wanted was the yellow butterfly... Perhaps the butterfly was tired of flying or simply wanted to give its wings to Isabel, because it sat quietly on the brown bark of a fallen araucaria. She too sat there in the silence, forgetting the thrill of the chase, until she noticed the contours of the butterfly were fading; it was already dusk and darkness had taken the place of shade. She was scared but she didn't scream and run wildly, only rocked her head to the secret murmur of the wind. Papa was sure to come looking for her with his torch and Mama, unable to suppress a sob, would wrap her in her shawl.

Then she heard a military truck rumble along the alley, approaching the house. They took her in like so many others who secretly dreamt of becoming condors and flying where no one had flown before.

There was so much regret in Isabel's voice that day in the woods, as if every time she opened the shutters to the past, memories poured in like lemon juice on an open sore. But they were so close then. He held her tight and she rubbed her face against his, burrowing a nest in his embrace, and he, as another with memories of tears frozen in his heart, felt the tears in her eyes. They were so silent, they could almost hear the dull throb of their pulses, and their footsteps fell into a rare harmony, as if they both knew exactly where they were going. Yet they were only wandering aimlessly among the yellow and brown leaves falling on the mossy ground. Then two wood pigeons flew out from a densely foliaged oak, rupturing the stillness of the afternoon.

At last he sits up in his bed, still wondering. Why hasn't she phoned? Perhaps something has happened to her, or perhaps he doesn't know her at all. What is she doing in London? Perhaps she went to a secret meeting of the underground cell; he doesn't know anything about it, but why should he? Isabel no doubt doesn't want to involve him. May be she has another lover. Damn you, Dulal, how can you think like that. Sometimes you can be so silly. But what is he to think? At least she could have rung once. Maybe she has sent him a note. It's only two days since she left, so a letter is unlikely, but wild hopes make him feel as if a letter is waiting for him. He trembles as if he is ripping it open in the gloom of the post-room and reading: Dear Dulal, so sorry to have left you without an explanation. I had to go away. I know you will forgive me, or am I being too presumptuous, compañero, to think that you will understand that the ghost of my past has come to claim me. Yours and my memories and ghosts, my darling, the same foolish dreams, although thousands of miles apart, are yet so close. I knew that you at least would understand. I knew you would; somehow we have always known it, your ghost and mine so close that we couldn't do anything else but turn away our faces. You haven't told me in so many words, but every time you scream in your sleep and I hold you tight, I know your ghost is claiming you, too. You see, Dulal, how can we not turn our faces and go the other way?

He can't bear it any longer, imagining the long torments and hearing her saying the final chao, because chao is the secret musk of the memory of that day when the sun came down to play, as it so rarely does, on the dank lawns of England. The clouds were so few and distant that they resembled tiny speckles of fish in the blue of a motionless sea. The fountain in the square – where students gather for indolent hours daydreaming of never-ending days like this – was spurting a crystal canopy of water. How clearly he still hears the rhythms of the water dropping in the pool, a sound that would have sent desert nomads delirious with dreams of paradise. Chequered awnings mushroomed in clusters everywhere, and under the shade of one, amidst laughter and drinks, he saw Isabel with her long brown hair, reading a book. How well he remembers the awkward moment when he came from behind and said hello. She looked up in a slight panic at the intrusion into her solitude, but somehow she found the right expression, as she always did, to greet him. He sat beside her and saw in the soft sepia of her eyes a strange familiarity floating over a pair of black holes, as if beneath the surface there was something of Isabel he mustn't intrude on. Yet all he wanted then was to drown himself in her eyes for ever. Suddenly Isabel caught a glimpse of her way of looking in the doubling mirror of his eyes, and it eased away the burden of her nightmares. Then they looked at each other as at someone they had always known. He remembers it clearly: there were two tall glasses of mineral water with ice, which they lifted with much expectation, as if each could sense the other's longing. And their parting *chao* was not a ceremony of good-bye but the promise of another meeting.

Almost believing a letter is waiting for him, he decides to get up, puts on his jeans and goes down to the post-room. Isabel must have written in her neat, flowing italics in blue ink, on that crisp see-through paper she loves so much, beginning abruptly, but never failing to write the *dear compañero*, each word inlaid with the perfume of her breath and an odd drop of sweat on the margin. He trembles to touch her, but no sign of a letter, not even a scrap of a note. He pauses for a minute against the dim, shadowy column of the post-room and allows himself memories of bitterness, the occasions when they got on each other's nerves and said cruel things. He sulks: how careless of her not to have written or phoned, she evidently doesn't give a damn about him, only her stupid obsession with the past and her guilt that she survived. She is too drowned in herself to think about him; all she wants is to do something, something really crazy, so that the nightmares won't haunt her any more. How soothing it is, Isabel, to be a bloody ghost among ghosts.

But it always ends with lighting a cigarette and blowing away the perverse pleasure of bitterness. He wonders what could have happened to her, hopes for her safety, even if she doesn't want to see him again. Yes, Isabel, you have reason enough to turn your face. I know I can't intrude into the opaque depths of your eyes. Your stories unfolded in another time and another place beyond me, yet when you look at me through the cloud that gathers in your eyes I see myself running the same way, on a parallel course, alongside you, compañera mia.

He envelopes himself in his long coat, lights another cigarette, and goes down the narrow pathway that leads to the main square of the campus where the fountain stands, and where in the summer he met Isabel reading a book. In this late morning, in the dull mood of a cold day, the square is deserted, except for two solitary figures at the far corner, perhaps postgraduates, playing chess on the giant open-air board. He wanders the length of the square, which expands as he moves, but he doesn't hurry, only ambles on with the delayed motion of a dromedary. When he looks up to orientate himself, he finds himself on the edge of the chessboard at whose ends the players stand motionless. They are almost hidden in their long black coats, and the enormous pieces remain in their pre-gambit squares, erect in their solitude and stillness like the players themselves. His presence, his shuffling legs, the hiss of the match when he lights a cigarette, fails to animate the players. He knows he can't be a part of their game but where else can he go? All those who had somewhere to go – the English and the local students – have already left for the Christmas vacation, leaving the foreigners the entire campus to themselves. Since they are not that many, and most of the facilities are shut, he can't do much other than make himself into the spectator of a game where neither the players nor the pieces ever seem to move.

None of this would have mattered, of course – rather he would have welcomed it – if Isabel were there. About the same time last year, he remembers, it was so nice when they were all alone together in the late morning in the coffee-bar, he having his tea and Isabel her coffee, sharing a newspaper between them. Isabel was mumbling her usual way through the pages, her mood changing from curiosity to outrage and then back to quiet reflection again. His mind wasn't on the newspaper but on what

she might surrender of herself in her changing moods. He
sipped at his tea quietly, content to observe her until she
assumed that alarming stillness that always reminded him of the
distance between them. He thought that if only he could catch
a faint murmur of that silence, the blankness of her face would
yield its secret, and he would finally know the story which
perhaps Isabel didn't know quite how to tell even herself.

Apart from her decision to go to London without an explanation, it is true that she has never kept any secret from him. It was
painful and it took time but she had told him how the tower and
the torture nearly broke her, and worst of all, how they had poked
her naked body as if she were a lump of dead meat. Whether it
was day or night she had no idea, but she knew that they were
squatting around her and smoking cigarettes, and poking her
with sticks as if they were little boys losing interest in the game.
You would think they would be wildly agitated, she told him, but
they were calm. For hours they talked among themselves about
the normal things that respectable people talk about when they
meet socially. A father talked tenderly about his daughter's
marriage, an old man about his wish for a motorbike because his
old legs couldn't make it up the hills any more, a kindly man
about fixing his neighbour's burst pipe, a pious man about the
mass he attended on Sunday. Whatever they talked, they talked
while smoking and poking her naked body as if she were dead
meat. He knows all this, but how can he know what Isabel really
felt? He didn't dare ask for more, for what could Isabel have said
that would have made any final sense. Even if he asked: Was
it their looking at you as if you were a dead frog, more than the
fear of death, that nearly broke you, Isabel? Even if she had
answered, Yes, how did you know? Truly, I wasn't scared of
dying, even when the fat guard with a kind face plunged my head
under that thick oily water and talked to one of the others about
his longing to go one day to the north, especially when the desert

was in bloom after the rains. He almost forgot me, but I didn't move, didn't give him a signal by raising my hand – not because I was brave, but it was like a dream. I was with my butterfly net following a yellow butterfly, and Mama, as usual, was doing her crochet on the veranda in the rocking chair, moving and rocking, and the idea of death never occurred to me. It was like a summer afternoon when your body gives in to the cooling breeze, and before you know where you are, you're already asleep. Yes, Dulal, it was the contempt in their eyes that nearly broke me.

But what good would it have done even if she had confirmed his feverish babbles? Would it have finally answered his terrible need to know how she really felt in those moments? Perhaps it was their echo that ran through Isabel every time she assumed that silence, her face so naked as to be almost without any expression. How painful it was that there were some parts of Isabel he could never reach, that she was more than all she could ever say to him. Now he curses himself for always returning to this blind spot that separates them so completely that they seem like creatures from different planets.

But why not remember the time last year when they were so happy together. After the coffee-bar they hitched a lift into town, full of people doing their last minute shopping. They hopped from shop to shop with the innocence of children in a glittery funfair; they could hardly believe themselves when they turned a blind eye to the Father Christmas promoting shoddy goods in a big store. What the hell, let's treat ourselves for a change! They bought a bottle of fine wine and top quality steaks. And there was the photo in the cubicle, Isabel sitting on his lap and pulling faces, her brown eyes, relieved of their burden of memories, shining and going out to meet him without the slightest reserve. That evening, Isabel fried the steaks, marinated in garlic and pepper, very well done for him. She teased him how a real connoisseur of steaks would be aghast seeing them so well done, and the rice and the hot pickle was a culinary travesty, but they were happy and the fruity tang of the full-bodied red wine brought laughter to Isabel's face. He even proposed a holiday and Isabel said, yes, perhaps they could go to a place where silvery sand met a blue lagoon fringed by palm-fronds hanging their green locks against a blue, blue sky. They lay side by side that night in their tiny bed, and turned the tape-recorder on; zampoña breathed from the very bowels of the earth and cascaded down the cordillera. When they entwined their bodies in embrace, their naked skin came so close as to touch the very membrane of their strangeness and the turning of the faces that would always be theirs. Why couldn't he accept that Isabel had to go away? Because she came so close? Yes, perhaps he should accept it, for it's the only way he can give himself to Isabel without reserve. Yes, but her memories of nightmares, if only he could immerse himself in the deep anguish of her soul, he could truly say, I know, Isabel, why you had to turn your face and go the other way.

But what is she doing in London? The underground cell must be sitting around in hushed silence. They don't need to say a word; the way they would look at her would remind her of her ghosts. It's time to go back, comrade. It would be that simple and clear, and Isabel would understand it without any ceremony and fuss. Your ghost is calling you back, Isabel, it claims you the way it has claimed others, that way at least you won't die with a guilty conscience.

He had known that much on the night of steaks and wine. After the music had stopped cascading down the cordillera and Isabel fell asleep, he had tossed and turned until he got up in the small hours of the night. There was moonlight and the long shadows of the pines stood in perfect symmetry across the field. How clearly he remembers that there wasn't the slightest flutter of a wind to ruffle the perfect symmetry. He had taken the rubble pathway to the lake, wishing to see the pairs of white swans, and there they were in their inseparable bonds, cruising among the speckled stars, so many of them that night reflected in the lake. He tried to imagine Isabel, to see her eyes when she gave herself away without reserve, but he couldn't see her face, she had already turned it away. He had come back, running. In the dark of the room, he'd touched Isabel's face, trying to remember its bony contours, but Isabel did not give her face to him; its geometry escaped him; he lost the face that was Isabel; she had become the condor again, flying high above the cordillera.

. Neither the players nor the pieces have moved yet, as if even the flutter of an eyelid would take years. He wishes he too could slow down his thoughts, yet they gather speed, because Isabel hasn't phoned him yet, not even a word. How could she do that to him? Perhaps she wants to protect him; he knows she wouldn't do anything that might harm him. No, she doesn't want to involve him in this mess – she has to do it all alone, yes, all alone. Why should she have any doubt about leaving it all behind? Especially not on account of these silly little attachments of exile. But would she think of him, while all alone in the tube, on her way to collect the ticket, and regret not having said goodbye to him properly? But that would only complicate matters; besides, the underground cell is so paranoid about security. It's best this way; at least she could treasure the moment when their skins came so close as to touch the membrane of their strangeness. Yes, compañero mio, you at least would understand why I had to turn my face. But does she search among the hollowed faces in the tube train's changing light and shadow between the stations for the face that came so naked to her and touched her wounds? Does she think, I know your ghosts claim you too – I know it every time you scream in your sleep and I hold you tight...? But how can she forget the tower? It's not just guilt, Dulal, I can't explain it... When the fat guard with the kind face

drowned me in the thick oily water, I fell in love with the silence,
Mama doing her crotchet on the veranda on the rocking chair,
moving and rocking, and the music, I never told you about that
music. When I'm alone or I close my eyes, it still rings in my
ears, not Mama's soft murmur in the evening shade, but the other
girl, the condor, whose face I have never seen. Her voice was so
clear, something really strange, I honestly don't know how to
describe it, but it always goes through me without meeting any
resistance. I should have told you about the nights, compañero,
especially when silence would descend on the tower, except for
the mechanical precision of the guards' footsteps pacing the
long corridor. She would hum and I would press my ears against
the wall to catch the echoes cascading down the cells and the
corridor of the tower. She still calls me out, the face I have never
seen calls me out, Dulal. How can I refuse her? I have to go. If
in your anger you call me damn stupid I would understand it, but
it's not just the fantasy of becoming a martyr. I want to live and
grow old like the old araucaria, dear compañero. I know you will
understand it, you are sure to understand it when you come face
to face with the ghosts that haunt you too.

Perhaps he should go to London to look for her, at least he
should phone Oscar and Kalpana. Isabel always stayed with
them in London, but if Isabel doesn't want to be found, they
wouldn't know a thing. Kalpana, with her aptitude for panic,
would think the worst, and Oscar, sensing what had happened,
would puff anxiously on his pipe and stay silent for so long that
he would forget the reason for his silence. Perhaps they would
to drive down from London to take him away for a break, to the
bleak hills of the Lake District, where so many poets walked to
tame the wild profusion of their anguish, and failed. And if he
went with Oscar and Kalpana to the Lake District, how could they
console him, what could they say that would make any sense?

Still trapped by the players, he wishes Isabel were here, how easily he could have broken away from this mindless game of chess. Almost involuntarily he gives himself to the feeling that Isabel is coming to him, tiptoeing from behind to surprise him. In that magical moment, facing the glint in her brown eyes, all the regrets and bitterness would melt away like a transient footprint on a shimmering sea of sand.

Suddenly, out of the grim sky, a flake of snow dances down the air and touches him on the tip of his nose. Ah this is his first snow in England; the flakes are swarming in packs and scattering and gliding down on the grey slabs of the square. But where is Isabel? Perhaps she is crossing Chelsea Bridge right now, along the left catwalk, between those white railings, under the glimmer of neon along the waterfront. There, one Spring, holding each other, they had strolled happily and then stood against the railings looking at London dancing a wild dance of light and breaking the seam that the fog had stitched around it. If she is there now, crossing the bridge, would she remember that moment? Perhaps, at this precise moment, Isabel is having her long brown hair strewn with white flakes of snow. He is sure that for her, too, this is her first snow in England. Perhaps she is standing against the railings again, this time in a desperate moment of regret. She wants to go back to him and accept her defeat and exile. She is thinking, Why not come face to face with him once again and dare to say, even if it is an illusion, aren't we so happy, Dulal? Yes, no doubt she would remember the scene from *Pather Panchali* which had come to her mind when she first saw him, and which she told him about so often. In that scene, Apu is washing his teeth with charcoal by the pond after Durga has died. The pond, where the rain played with the water lilies, now resonates with the quiet desolation on Apu's face. Perhaps he is remembering the day they went to see the train, running through the forest of wild grasses with their canopy of white flowers moving ever so gently in the breeze. Apu was scared then, but Durga lovingly encouraged her little brother, leading him on to put their ears on the tracks to listen to the vibrations going further and further away before disappearing. Perhaps it was that happy memory that made Apu look so sad by the pond. It is this sad face of Apu that looks at Isabel every time she remembers him. It is summoning her now, but the girl who hummed in the tower, whose face she had never seen, has an immemorial claim on her. Besides, the underground cell has ordered her to go back. She has to go back. Perhaps right now she is leaning over the railings and looking at the floating filaments of light bouncing off the pitch-dark surface of the water, perhaps glancing one last time at the butt-end of the cigarette she has just flicked over the railings, which is falling like a wounded firefly. She would overcome her desire to return to him, and walk away, as if he had already become a distant memory among so many sad memories.

Dulal walks across the square towards the coffee-bar, which is now open for a few hours to serve the foreign students. Outside the flakes are growing in number, becoming almost like showers of cotton-wool from tall kapok trees. Mr. Lung, his enigmatic neighbour, who always dips out of sight before he can say, *Hi Mr. Lung*, comes rushing towards him. He is so happy to see the snow, asks Dulal how he likes it, grins and disappears again. He walks into the coffee-bar, where they have spent so many happy hours together, now looking cold and empty. He buys himself a sandwich and a tea. Outside, the snow is continuing to fall. What is Isabel doing at this moment? Perhaps she is making her last minute preparations for the flight home and dreaming of condors again, but what can he do about it? Nothing, absolutely nothing. So he imagines Isabel as a little girl. She is sitting by the window, looking at the snowcapped peaks of the mountains, stainless white against the spotless blue of the sky. Isabel's mama calls her – *Isabel, oh Isabel, my pretty darling, where are you? Want to come to the market with Mama?* She doesn't answer, she just leans over to clean a patch on the dusty sill with her long sleeves. Her mama, hearing no response, thinks that the child is day-dreaming again, so she goes to the market, leaving her alone by the window. Isabel now feels the lush moments of solitude ticking by, which only heightens her longing to see a condor gliding up and up until it becomes blurred in the blue of the sky. Today, for some strange reason, there isn't any condor in the sky. Perhaps a guanaco has misjudged its nimble footwork at a precipice and the condors are swarming at the bottom of some deep ravine for the rich pickings. This explanation does not satisfy her though; on the contrary, her longing for condors only becomes more acute. She invents with wonderment and delight the flapping grey wings cutting a winding path, slowly and silently going further and further away. Her mama comes back from the market. She asks, *What's the matter with you darling? Aren't you feeling well?* Isabel brings herself to say, *I'm fine, Mama,* and looks out of the window again, now imagining the circular descendings of the condors, no more than specks of dust to begin with, then dropping smoothly, the span of the wings now revealing their immensity against the tranquil density of blue. Her mama comes rushing in because she too hears the flapping of wings, Isabel's and the condor's. Mama stands in the door-way, looking at the condor, too lost even to let out a tiny cry of amazement, stands there looking at the condor in the room bathed in the muted glow of the evening.

He walks to the counter for another cup. Meanwhile, two students have entered the bar and are playing on the pinball machine. He goes back to his seat, lights a cigarette and goes over the scene in which Isabel leaves for London. It is all there: Isabel not able to look him in the eyes, the burning cigarette between her tense, trembling fingers. She was going for good. He knows that now but why couldn't she tell him as much? Of course, he would have been upset, it's only natural, but in the end, if Isabel had wanted to go, he would have let her. Perhaps, though, it had nothing to do with not getting him involved in a mess, perhaps she just couldn't face the idea of another good-bye, feeling it better to leave without any ceremony. Saying goodbye would only have exposed her vulnerability to tears. Perhaps she could have coped with that, but how could she have left him with tears in his eyes? But how is he to understand all that? Do the images of Isabel as a little girl dreaming of condors, imprisoned in the Tower, following the yellow butterfly and becoming a condor herself, give him any clues as to why she had to turn her face and go the other way?

The two students who have been playing on the pin ball machine approach him for a light. It doesn't take them long to sense his loneliness, so they invite him for a game. He vaguely remembers them, students like himself from distant continents, but he declines their kind gesture. Now feeling uneasy, because he is aware that they are sniffing his desolation with the sensitivity of dogs, he slinks out of the coffee bar into the square again. He is relieved to see that the chess players have gone. The snow hasn't stopped falling, and the black pieces are gathering flakes around their bodies and becoming white, facing the white pieces on a board already under heaps of snow. As one not used to snow, he moves cautiously. Isabel wouldn't have found it difficult, because she is not unfamiliar with snow. She had seen her condors against the backdrop of the snowcapped cordillera, perhaps soon to be seen again. Will it make it worthwhile, will it ease the pain of separation, Isabel? If only you could answer this simple question for me, my dear compañera, things would have been a bit clearer, and I could have taken my tea remembering that autumn afternoon when we walked through the mauve woods. I know the condors will be happy; they will soar and soar on their giant wings to heights they have never soared before, because Isabel has returned to the fold. But I fear for you, Isabel, because I know that the guard with the kind face – who perhaps now rides a brand new Kawasaki – will be waiting for you. He will watch you through the black tint of his sun glasses – I wouldn't be surprised if he can see through the dark of the night. I bet he won't be in a hurry to claim you. Perhaps he will allow himself the dream of going to the north again when the desert's in bloom. He knows your ghost has already claimed you, as so many others have been claimed.

When it was, he can't remember, but he's sure that it was after a party where they danced to the wailing of deep rub-a-dub that throbbed from the very roots of the trees, moving their lethargic limbs to minimalist undulation, where there had been an endless supply of drinks well into the night. Afterwards, they had walked to their place under a cool crispy sky, Isabel so drunk he almost had to drag her. He had put her to bed and sat by the window to smoke a cigarette. Then he heard her mumbling barely audibly, as if speaking to herself, words without any narrative thread to tie them, but each one of them spoken as if from some unspeakable depths. He couldn't pick them all up, but *cordillera*, *condor*, *cactus* and *copper* insisted on him by their sheer repetition.

When he got up the next morning he didn't ask her what stories these words might be telling, because he couldn't face up to what might be hiding in their dark fissures. These words had already penetrated deep into his body, yet they were so hard he had never dared to break them open and tell himself the story that Isabel, despite herself, might have told him that night. Now he tells himself that it must be a place where rain never falls, as dry as dinosaur bones, where not even a desert nomad breaks the monotony of light and wind. Closed in upon itself, it is a place given over to the play of rocks and volcanic lava. Isabel had a thing about the desert, but not, of course, in bloom, when the profusion of colour robs it of its singular passion for a greyish brown that goes on and on to infinity. Her dreams are of a desert without flowers where, amidst the solitary cacti and the symphony of light and wind, she can set her foot without coming across a previous footprint, as a true nomad of the desert.

But now it is no longer a dream. She has been taken to the desert she so often dreamt of with the clear eyes of a condor. For a moment she tries to tell herself that if the circumstances were different, she would have been over the moon with it. Now she is huddled on a military bus with many others; without exception they are blindfolded. Nothing but the heat and dust in the silence and the smell of salt drones on her the proximity of the desert. The prisoners drown themselves in their own thoughts; nobody asks the person next to him or her who they are and where they have come from. These questions do not matter any more; they are heading for the same anonymous death in the desert, nothing more to know, only memories of the past. The soldiers who clapped and sang and cracked jokes much of the way are silent too. Only the whirring of the motor prevents complete silence. Then the bus comes to a halt. She hears the soldiers getting off one by one, forming a file and marching off. When the drilled precision of their footfalls disappears in the distance, Isabel at last finds herself in the silence she has always craved like an addict's fix, and she wonders if the guard who dreams of going to the north to see the desert in bloom is one of those who marched off. Is he going to have the same kind face when he pulls the trigger, or will he be bitter with disappointment because there is no bloom in the desert? It is a long while since the soldiers left, but the prisoners are still blindfolded, and are silent as ever. Suddenly Isabel feels the urge to say something to the body next to her, but words elude her. She wishes her hands were not tied, that she could touch the body next to her and commune with it. Then she hears the hum, the same clear voice that went through her every time she heard it in the tower. The girl whose face she has never seen is the body next to hers; she is humming again, the condor is humming. Isabel leans her body to touch the girl, and the girl rests her head on Isabel's shoulder, but they don't speak to each other. They don't need to speak to each other, because everything between them is spoken in the touch of their bodies. The girl is still humming and Isabel is falling asleep, dreaming of condors spreading their wings and soaring higher and higher until they disappear in the blue. Then the soldiers return, stamping their boots on the ground. They are shouting at the prisoners and pushing them off the bus. But where is the girl, Isabel wonders; she is no longer next to her. She knows her by her smell, and it is not her smell on the body next to hers. First the soldiers line the prisoners up and link their bodies with ropes, pulling them along under the hot sun of the desert. Isabel feels her feet burning on the dry bone of the desert; she longs for shade and a cool breeze to lull her to sleep, never to wake again. Finally, the soldiers are leading them down a curve, perhaps to a disused copper mine, because Isabel can smell the strong salty tang of copper ore. They are at the bottom now; it is cool in the shade. The solders untie the ropes, line the prisoners up sideways. In front, another group of solders is taking up position with their automatic rifles. Isabel wishes the girl whose face she hasn't seen would hum again, but she doesn't. One of the prisoners shouts, *Take my blindfold off, I want to see the sky*, but the solders ignore him as if he is already dead. They are getting on with their task with the meticulous precision of finely tuned machines. They are checking their weapons, loading the magazines with bullets. Why doesn't the condor hum? Perhaps she is dreaming her own memories. Isabel feels drowsy in the cool shade of the mine, she is following the yellow butterfly again and getting lost under the dark canopy of the forest, carried away by the secret murmur of the wind. Papa must be drowning himself under piles of work, staying up late, but he will look at the stars and hope that he will find her, the way he once found her with his torch light. And poor Mama must be doing her crochet on the veranda, in the rocking chair, moving, rocking until the sky turns dark and she can't see any more. When the officer gives the order, Isabel does not hear it, only the faint sound of the bullets. She has already fallen to the ground, many other bodies on top of her. What expression does the guard with the kind face bear on his face now? Is he bitter because there is no bloom in the desert, only light and wind in the endless waste as dry as dinosaur's bones? Isabel feels the blood, showers of blood, bathing her for a journey so speeded up until everything comes to a standstill. When Isabel opens her eyes she realises she is not dead; she lies under the bodies for a long time, wishing to fall asleep again, then remembers the girl who communed with her on the bus, softly touched her beneath her skin and marked her with the eternal force of trembling. She pushes aside the bodies and gets up, because she must find the face of the girl before it is too late. She takes her blindfold off and rummages among the bodies, touching their faces, but she cannot remember the geometry of the girl's face, because she has never touched it. She wonders what lines, what contours, what curves she should look for. Then she remembers the smell, and she takes each body in her arms and rubs her nose against their skins. But they all smell the same, the cold of death mingled with the salt of the desert. She has lost her for good among the bodies, which are as anonymous as the rocks and the volcanic lava of the desert. Isabel crawls out of the mine. The soldiers have left some time ago; perhaps the mechanical diggers will come later in the night to bury the bodies. Once out of the mine, she runs over the flat expanse of the desert, looking for water. Somewhere in the distance she sees sunlight playing on a milk-white pool of water.

She rushes to it, but it is a only a mirage, sun reflected by the dry salt of the lake. In desperation, she digs with her bare hands until she collapses with exhaustion. Lying on the salt lake, she looks at the cordillera, snowcapped in the distance. Then she sees the grey wings of the condors, cutting a winding path up, gliding down and circling above her.

Now that he has told himself the story, will it finally explain why Isabel had to turn her face and go the other way? No. Because the unknown face of the girl summons Isabel in a different way from his own melancholy face. She calls out to Isabel to justify her indolent days of exile, her thesis, her love, and her dreams of a career. Perhaps Isabel couldn't justify herself any longer. He knows that the unknown face of the girl has finally claimed her, taken her back to the fold where the guard with the kind face will be waiting for her with the infinite patience of an anaconda. However callous, even he couldn't fail to feel pity for crazies like her who, for god knows what reason, came back to die.

Dulal is going round and round the square, his hair and his long coat getting covered with snow, but moving ever more slowly, because he doesn't want to arrive anywhere any more. Besides, he senses that the horizon is pushed so far in the distance that all attempts to reach it would be futile. Has Isabel taken the plane yet? Or perhaps right now she is walking along the Embankment, where once they walked together and waited to listen to Big Ben calling out the hours. They were so childishly happy then. Perhaps she will be tempted to call him on the phone. *Dulal, compañero mio, what am I to do, I haven't called you before because I couldn't bear the idea of saying chao to you for the last time. Your face calls me so strongly I feel like flying back to you.* If she had really called him and said these things, he would be silent and wouldn't insist on her coming back, because he would know now that the unknown face of the girl had already claimed her.

Mr. Lung sees him circling around. He says: *You like snow so much? You want to be a snowman or what?* Dulal doesn't know what to say in response. He is surprised by Lung's boldness. Perhaps he should have laughed at his joke, but he has forgotten how to laugh. Together they walk back to the hall of residence. Lung asks: *Your friend, where is she?* He tells him: *She is in London.* Lung doesn't ask any more questions, perhaps he has sensed that something is wrong. He walks quietly beside him as if he wants simply to be his friend in his hour of need. Lung says: *I'll cook a duck tonight, we can eat together, yes?* Dulal thanks him and accepts. When they arrive at Lung's flat on the fifteenth floor, Lung makes tea for both of them. They sit in the kitchen, take their tea and look out through the big glass window. Snow is still falling; the grounds are completely white. He lights a cigarette and imagines what would have happened if Isabel were here to share this moment with him. Perhaps she would have dragged him out in the snow and they would have played snowballs like children. Lung tells Dulal he will call him in the evening when the dinner is ready. He thanks Lung and goes back to his room.

What else to do? He browses through his books; nothing grabs his attention; perhaps he should be working on his thesis. Is Isabel at the airport now? Perhaps the flight's delayed because of the snow. If she has any doubt, she wouldn't dare reveal it to the underground cell; they would look at her with pity for such weakness. Once the cell had decided that the cadres must go back, nothing else would matter. But why can't he let Isabel go, why can't he accept what they have always known between them? Isabel had to turn her face one day. Now that he has told himself the story of what happened in the desert, everything should have become clear.

How not to remember the vigil for the Disappeared they attended in London – the grimness of it all? On a drizzly night, down in a crypt, beneath low vaults, between thick colonnades, they had moved among clusters of figures who stood in motionless murmurs. He had wanted to turn back, because he couldn't bear the shadows and the ghostly lights fluttering dimly from the niches. He knew that he would lose Isabel among the masses of grains, those black and white photographs enlarged from less than perfect copies. Yes, he'd been right. Isabel had stood before each portrait as if trying to look through the grains, as if she might conjure up the unknown face of the girl. He knew then that her ghost had claimed her.

He lies in his bed with his clothes on, turns on the radio: snow is falling all over the country; it will fall throughout the night. He turns the radio off, pulls the quilt over him, then he remembers the photo, taken last year when they were in town, of Isabel sitting on his lap, pulling faces, giving her brown eyes without the slightest reserve. Is it going to be the only token of what was between them? He must phone Oscar and Kalpana; they are bound to have some news. Although nothing was said in so many words, he always assumed that Oscar was linked to the cell. He rushes down to the telephone, dials the number; Kalpana answers at the other end. They have no news of Isabel, but Kalpana is worried and insists that he comes to London. He mustn't stay on his own at a time like this. If Oscar hadn't gone away to a conference he would have come for him in the car. Kalpana stays silent for a long time, she doesn't know what else to say, she is already thinking the worst, that something terrible must have happened to Isabel. Suddenly she says, her voice about to break into pieces, *Promise me, Dulal, you will come to London. Isabel, poor Isabel, I wish I were a believer like my mother and could pray that everything will be fine*. He senses that Kalpana's eyes are getting misty, so he promises her everything she wants to hear. Yes, he will come to London, but he doesn't mean to, not because he wants to avoid the awkwardness of having to deal with

Kalpana's tears, but because it might break open the torrent of
tears mutely raging within himself. When he hangs up, he
regrets having misled Kalpana, but what could he do? If only
Isabel had phoned and cleared up the whole mess, everybody
could have vented their anguish and then got on with their lives.
He stays around the telephone. If he hears her voice at the other
end, he would be relieved, perhaps angry too. *Why have you
made me suffer so much, you know how anxious I get. The worst
part of it, Isabel, is not knowing what has happened to you.* How
would Isabel respond to his bitter words? Perhaps she wouldn't
say anything to defend herself, perhaps in her silence he would
come to recognise the anguish she carried in her heart, the silent
agony of not knowing what had happened to the girl whose face
she has never seen, the girl whose face she searched for among
the grainy photographs of the disappeared. Even if Isabel
doesn't phone or write to him, in time he will stop feeling angry,
because he knows he is coming to understand the anguish Isabel
has been feeling all this time.

   He goes back to his room, lights a cigarette, looks out through
chinks in the curtain. It is still snowing. All the previous colours
of the fields are now veiled with luminous whiteness, as if the
blooms of lilies have taken over the earth. He sees a rabbit
making its tracks on the maiden snow, its footprints going up the
little mound and coming down again. How he wishes that Isabel
had made these footprints, or at least had been there to see the
rabbit. He remembers how Isabel always looked out of this
window whenever a depressive mood weighed on her, whenever
her ghost came to claim her. Perhaps she is now released from
that torment, perhaps right now she is looking out of the window
of the plane, relaxed because she has finally responded to the
summons so mournfully whispered by the girl whose face she
has never seen. Perhaps, though, she is looking out at the clouds
burdened by another face, but this time by the face that always

reminded her the face of Apu by the pond, saddened by the memories of Durga.

Mr. Lung knocks on the door. In fact, he has been knocking for some time. *Are you all right?* he asks, but without betraying any sense of serious concern. Dulal opens the door and explains that he had just dozed off. Together they go to the kitchen where Lung has already cooked the duck and laid the table. Outside, darkness has fallen. Though they can't see the snow any more, they know that it is still falling. They are calling it the heaviest fall in years, informs Lung. Dulal brings cans of lager from his fridge and puts them on the table, but Lung doesn't drink, so he has to drink them all himself. While he opens a can and licks the froth that bubbles out, Lung serves the duck with plain, fragrant rice together with Chinese cabbage, chilli sauce, and dark, dense, liquid soya. Between mouthfuls, they pause long to talk about the distant places they have left to come here, remember the flavours of their fruits in season, the rivers that swell to pour over the land, the rain that continues for days. How strange is the snow in this strange land, yet they have longed for it intensely. Then Lung brings the subject up so casually, as if he hasn't given it a second thought.

– *Is your girlfriend... is she not coming back?*

– *I don't know anything, Lung. Honestly, I don't even know whether she has left or not, I don't know anything.*

After that they remain silent. Lung searches for something to say to cheer him up, but he can't find anything suitable for the occasion. Dulal, drinking his lager between pieces of duck and rice, drifts to his own thoughts. When they finish the meal, he helps Lung with the washing up and thanks him for everything, for his kindness and concern. He goes back to his room with the remaining cans of lager.

He finishes the lager and the packet of cigarettes and peers through the chinks between the splashes of snow on the window.

In the dim light from the lamp he sees that the snow has stopped falling now. He takes off his clothes, goes under the quilt, puts on the cassette-player and pulls the quilt like a cylinder around him. He hears the sounds of the zampoña cascading down the cordillera and wonders why Isabel didn't take the music with her. Is it to remind him of that night when they rose from their bodies and went the other way together? I remember that night, Isabel, and I long for your face the way you long for the unknown face of the girl you lost in the desert. Yet how am I to understand the way you have turned your face? Perhaps if I had known the tower, and the guard with the kind face had poked me as if I were a piece of dead meat, or if I had looked for your face in the desert among unknown faces, or perhaps if I could unlock that other story, which you never knew, yet to which you drew my attention so often – *Dulal, my poor darling, every time you wake up screaming in the night and I hold you tight, I know your ghost is claiming you too* – perhaps then I could have given you what you so mournfully demanded of me. Yes, Isabel, I know I have to come face to face with the ghost of my own nightmares, perhaps only then will I be able to come to terms with your disappearance, and love you and search for you the way you have loved and searched for the face you have lost in the desert. The cassette ends and the sounds of the zampoña disappear like the swish of the condor in the blue.

It is early in the morning and somebody is knocking on the door. It is Mr. Lung. He is calling Dulal because there is a phone call for him. Lung doesn't know who it is, but it is a female voice for sure, and she sounded kind of anxious. Dulal leaps out of his bed, slips into his jeans, and grabs his long coat. In the lift he thinks, *It's Isabel, I knew she would phone; she knows how anxious I get*. What would she say? Of course, *dear compañero*, to begin with, then perhaps sensing that he was a bit offended she would say: *How can you think that I would turn my face from you and disappear. How could I erase your scream from the red fluid of my body? Forgive me, compañero mio, for leaving you in the dark for the last few days.* But if he asks, *Why, Isabel, why did you do that?* How would she answer? Anyway, what does it matter, he tells himself, because he doesn't care for explanations any more. Now he imagines that Isabel is returning, that she is asking him to meet her at the station. He closes his eyes, seeing Isabel getting off the train, her long brown hair flying in the wind. She is looking at him without the slightest reserve and their lips meet without a word between them. They will touch each other's faces, at first slowly then quickly, but over and over again, until they have inscribed their elusive geometry in the depths of their souls for ever. Nothing will escape, not a single line or contour of a bone, and that way, if they are ever lost in the dark, they will always be able to find each other simply by touching each other's faces. Isabel is returning to him, and bringing him a present, because she never forgets to bring him presents. Perhaps it will be an alpaca cap this time, especially now that it is snowing.

Out of the lift, he rushes to pick up the phone. It is not Isabel but Kalpana. She has no news of Isabel but insists that he must come to London. In her voice a dark mood has set in. *The worst part of it is not knowing what has happened to her*, says Kalpana, trembling. *Yes Kalpana*, he agrees. *If only I knew what has happened, no matter how bad the news was. I would have been sad, of course, very sad, but then in time, who knows, even I could have accepted that Isabel has gone for good.*

He puts on his long coat, lights a cigarette and takes the narrow pathway that leads to the main square of the campus, where one summer he met Isabel reading a book. Now that the square is under the reign of snow, even the immobile players of chess have departed. Nothing to detain him in the square, he slowly wanders towards the field, over the unsoiled mass of lilies. He looks at the rows of conifers. How strange they look in their veils of snow. Blinded by the luminous lilies, he begins to circle the conifers, round and round until he feels dizzy and falls to the ground. He lies face-up. Once again the snow is falling and covering his face. Yes, let the lilies cover him. But how can he face up to the ghosts of his nightmares? I know, Isabel, every time I get up screaming and you hold me tight, my ghosts are trying to claim me too. No, I don't let them claim me, you see, that's why I get up screaming. I don't want to remember them, Isabel, because they are full of screams and the odour of fresh blood. But what other way is there for me? I have to remember them, otherwise how can I ever accept your departure without feeling bitterness, and long for you like you long for the unknown face of the girl. I owe you at least one story, Isabel. I have never told you a story, have I?

Truly Isabel, there are so many, I don't know where to begin. Perhaps this one, I will tell you this one. That afternoon it rained so much the fields were flooded. We thought they weren't going to come that day because they didn't like rain. So we didn't go to the mango groves to hide as we had been doing for months. We were so relaxed, we forgot to be vigilant. We hadn't seen our sisters and mothers for months, because they'd had to sail across the great swamp, to the heart of the labyrinth, where the soldiers would never find them. We missed our mothers and sisters but they had to be sent away, because the last time the army came they burnt down our houses, killed many of us and violated the bodies of many mothers and sisters. Perhaps, I should tell you this story, Isabel, but I don't know how to tell it yet, because it is too painful for me. I don't want to remember it, not even in my dreams. You see, Isabel, every time I get up screaming and you hold me tight, I fight with the memories of that event. Sure, they want to be remembered, but the screams... and... no, I can't remember them. No matter how abjectly they beg me to allow

them to come, I always push them away. I get up screaming so
that they couldn't sneak into me while I sleep. Sorry, Isabel, I
can't tell you that story yet.

That day when it rained so much that we didn't go to the
mango groves to hide – I think I told you this much – we boys
were playing games in the huts that we built after our homes were
burnt down. We were happy because we believed they wouldn't
come on a day like this. Our elder brothers and fathers went to
fish in the swamp. They caught so many that they had to carry
them the way they carry sheaves of ripened rice. We boys sat
watching in a circle. Our elder brothers and fathers cooked the
fishes in clay pots. We all ate together on the smooth green of the
banana leaves. It was so delicious; our first proper meal in
months. We ate so much that we had to lie down on the spot and
sleep. When we got up in the afternoon, it was still raining. And
when we heard the fakir strumming his two-stringed dootara, we
gathered around him. Seeing us around him, he lifted himself up
from the floor, drawing melody from his dootara. Some of the
brothers and fathers tapped on clay pots. While the fakir whirled
around singing, the rest of us clapped. We had no idea that the
hut was surrounded. When we heard the officer ordering us to
come out one by one, holding our hands on our heads, it was
already too late. I don't know why, but they separated us boys
from our elder brothers and fathers. Anyway, they tied our
hands, forming a small column. But they lined our elder brothers
and fathers up against the hut. Rain water came up to their
ankles, touching the edges of their lungies. The officer ordered
his men not to waste any bullets, so they used only bayonets. The
rest I don't remember, except for the screams and the blood that
flowed on the water. No, Isabel, I'm not telling you the truth, I
do remember everything, but I don't know how to tell it, not even
to myself.

He is still lying face-up in the snow. Lilies are falling and their white petals are covering his face. He senses that someone is coming his way; he can feel the footsteps on the snow. But there is something else. A dog runs past him, panting. Perhaps the owner has thrown a ball and the dog is running after it, but the dog comes back and licks his face. Seeing the dog stop for no apparent reason, the owner calls it back, but it hesitates to leave him. The owner calls it again, but this time with much more force, and the dog runs away, its footsteps disappearing in the distance. He is alone again and the petals of lilies are still falling on his face. *Isabel, compañera mia, my ghosts claim me too, the faces of my brothers and fathers and mothers and sisters. What are we to do then? Turn our faces from each other and dream of the moment when our skins came so close as to touch the very membrane of our strangeness? I don't know anything; perhaps it doesn't matter any more. Now that you made me tell you one of my stories, Isabel, I can accept your going away without any bitterness, because I now know with what force the girl whose face you have never seen calls you out. She calls you out the way you call me out. I long for your face the way you long for her face. Fly away condorita, fly away, I can hear the swish of your wings; you are touching the blue, touch the blue.*